TJ and the TIME STUMBLERS

BOOK 1
New Kid Catastrophes

Bill Myers

Tyndale House Publishers, Inc.
Carol Stream, Illinois

Visit Tyndale's exciting Web site for kids at www.tyndale.com/kids.

Visit Bill Myers's Web site at www.billmyers.com.

TYNDALE and Tyndale's quill logo are registered trademarks of Tyndale House Publishers, Inc.

New Kid Catastrophes

Designed by Stephen Vosloo

Edited by Sarah Mason

Published in association with the literary agency of Alive Communications, Inc., 7680 Goddard Street, Suite 200, Colorado Springs, CO 80920, www.alivecommunications.com.

Scripture quotations are taken from the *Holy Bible*, New Living Translation, copyright © 1996, 2004, 2007 by Tyndale House Foundation. Used by permission of Tyndale House Publishers, Inc., Carol Stream, Illinois 60188. All rights reserved.

For manufacturing information regarding this product, please call 1-800-323-9400.

Library of Congress Cataloging-in-Publication Data

Myers, Bill, date.
   New kid catastrophes / Bill Myers.
    p. cm. — (TJ and the time stumblers ; bk. 1)
   Summary: After she accidentally makes an enemy of superstar Hesper Breakahart on her first day at Malibu Junior High, thirteen-year-old TJ's troubles multiply when two twenty-third century students, who have traveled back in time to observe her for a history project, decide to help her.
   ISBN 978-1-4143-3453-0 (sc)
   [1. Junior high schools—Fiction. 2. Schools—Fiction. 3. Friendship—Fiction. 4. Time travel—Fiction. 5. Malibu (Calif.)—Fiction.] I. Title.
   PZ7.M98234New 2011
   [Fic]—dc22   2010047368

Printed in the United States of America

17   16   15   14   13   12   11
7   6   5   4   3   2   1

For Bruce Grimm . . .
whose humor I've never forgotten

Prologue

"This is outloopish, dude!" Herby shouted. "We're in the wrong century!"

"Actually," Tuna argued, "according to my expert calculations, we have landed precisely where we intended in Malibu, California, during the 21st century."

Herby looked out the window of their tiny time-travel pod. "Are you sure?"

"I am sure."

"Then you might want to mention that to the giant Tyrannosaurus rex."

"What giant Tyrannosaurus rex?"

"The one that's about to eat us."

"Don't be ridiculous." Tuna sighed. "There's no Tyrannosaurus—"

Normally he would have finished his sentence, but it's hard finishing sentences when you're drowned out by a very loud and very bloodcurdling

RAH**HrRRR**...

which, of course, is the sound all hungry Tyrannosaurus rexes make just before they start eating. (It's kinda like saying the blessing, but without all the head bowing, talking to God, and amen stuff.)

Herby looked at Tuna.

Tuna looked at Herby.

Then both boys did what they do best. They

"**AuGG**HHHH!"

screamed for their lives.

"Hit reverse!" Herby yelled. "Get us out of here!"

Herby didn't have to ask twice (actually he didn't have to ask once) because Tuna was already resetting the time pod's coordinates. Stomping on the gas, he

WHOOoosh-ed . . .

them through time to the 21st century, where they originally wanted to go.

That was the good news.

Unfortunately there was a little bad news, and it sounded exactly like

chug-a-chug-a

choke-a-**choke**-a

cough-**cough**-cough . . .

"What's that?" Herby asked.

"The sound all time-travel pods make when they run out of fuel."

"Out of fuel?!" Herby cried.

"Relax," Tuna said, glancing out his window. "As you can clearly see, we've safely arrived at the proper coordinates."

Herby opened his window to get a better view. It was true—Malibu beach was just 100 feet below them and 350 feet to the right. "Whew," he sighed, "we could have been majorly zworked."

"Yes, we could have," Tuna agreed.

"So just steer us over to the beach and let's land this thing."

"I would love to, however . . ."

"However what?"

"There is still that unfortunate problem of

chug-a-chug-a ***choke**-a-**choke**-a* *cough-**cough**-cough . . .*

running out of fuel."

"Which means?"

"Which means we are about to drop into the Pacific Ocean like a rock."

Herby turned to Tuna and swallowed. "When?"

"If my calculations are correct, I'd say right about

No**w!!**"

SpLAsH!

Fortunately, an automatic life raft inflated around the time pod. So other than the 847 gallons of sea-water pouring in through Herby's open window, they were perfectly safe. Now it was just a matter of paddling the pod to shore, turning on their cloaking device so no one would see them, and beginning their assignment.

There was, however, one other sound they had not counted on.

crinkle-crinkle

krackle-krackle

zit-zit pop

"What's that?" Herby asked.

"Nothing much."

"And by 'nothing much,' you mean—"

"The sound of all our electrical equipment shorting out from 847 gallons of seawater pouring over it."

"Is that all?" Herby said. "I thought we were in major trouble."

"Oh, we are," Tuna said. "We're in major trouble, big-time."

CHAPTER ONE

Beginnings . . .

TIME TRAVEL LOG:

Malibu, California, October 9

Begin Transmission:

21st-century education is majorly weird. Kids sit
in boring rooms listening to boring grown-ups talk
about boring subjects. What a torked way to learn.
Have encountered subject. She's as smoot as her
holographs in the history museum. Soon she will
encounter Chad Steel, her next-door neighbor.
Bummer, 'cause she really is smoot. I think Tuna
is in love. Me too. She's smooted to the max!

End Transmission

"TJ, look out!"

Thelma Jean Finkelstein glanced up just in time to see the family's grand piano racing toward her. The moving guys were rolling it down the ramp of the moving van. Well, they *had* been rolling it. Now it was rolling itself, faster than a speeding bullet with TJ as the target.

The way she figured, she had three choices:

CHOICE #1—Become piano roadkill.

CHOICE #2—Leap to the left and into the pool. Usually no prob—she loved swimming (except her hair always frizzed out). The problem today was the pool was empty and she was near the deep end. Deep as in, *call the ambulance, 'cause she'll be breaking both of her legs* kinda deep.

CHOICE #3—Leap to the right. Again, no prob, except for that pesky sliding glass door. Somehow, regaining consciousness while attendants picked broken glass out of her hair (in that same ambulance) was not how she wanted to spend her first day in Malibu, California.

This left TJ with Choice #4. (I know she figured three choices, but she's never been good at math.) The ever-popular *leap on top of the gas barbecue and hope the piano somehow misses you* choice.

A great idea. Except the piano didn't somehow miss her . . . or the barbecue. Instead, it sort of

CRASH-ed

into the barbecue and sent TJ flying into the air.

Actually, the flying part was easy. It was the landing that wasn't so great. The good news was she didn't land in the pool or slam into the sliding glass door. The bad news was she landed on top of the piano . . . which was still rolling . . . straight toward the neighbors' fence!

By now her whole family had run around the house to see what all the hysterical screaming and pants-wetting was about.

Dad was giving his usual Dad advice: "TJ, quit fooling around and get off that piano this instant!"

Little six-year-old Dorie was jumping up and down shouting in her cute little six-year-old voice, "Yippee! Can I go next? Can I go next?"

Nine-year-old Violet (part-time genius and

full-time pain in the neck) was already scheming.
"If she dies, can I have her room?"

And what family get-together would be complete without Fido the Wonder Dog barking his little wonder-dog head off?

TJ would have loved to stick around and chitchat with everyone, but it's hard chitchatting when you're hanging on for your life and screaming your lungs out.

And the fun and games weren't exactly over. She still had to introduce herself to the neighbors. Unfortunately, this involved having to

SMASH

through their fence and join the little pool party they were having.

Fortunately, they were kids her age and probably attended the same school she'd be starting tomorrow.

Unfortunately, they were kids her age and probably attended the same school she'd be starting tomorrow.

Sigh . . .

Of course, the guests did the usual screaming and shouting. "Run for your lives; it's a crazy girl riding a piano!" But they didn't have to worry. Their pool was full of water, which explains the

SPLASH

of the grand piano . . . and the

glug . . . glug . . . glug

of its sinking to the bottom. (With luck this would mean no piano lessons till Dad bought another one . . . or at least till he got TJ some cool scuba gear.)

She thought of sticking around and swimming a few laps (to work off that extra pizza she had for lunch), but there was something about 20 rich and snobbish 13-year-olds all staring down at her that made her change her mind.

Then there was the most gorgeous boy she'd ever seen in her life. He was stooping down and reaching out his hand to her.

"Hey, are you all right?" he asked.

After coughing up a gallon of water, she nodded and took his hand.

"I'm Chad," he said. "Chad Steel."

She climbed out of the pool, a droopy, drippy mess, and looked into his incredible blue eyes.

He grinned. "It looks like we're neighbors."

She nodded, unable to take her eyes from his.

He kept smiling. "And your name is?"

She wanted to introduce herself but was having a hard time finding her voice, much less remembering her name. (Incredible blue eyes will do that to a person.)

He cocked his head, waiting for an answer.

Come on, TJ, she thought. (*It is TJ, isn't it?*)

His smile sagged a little.

It was now or never. She opened her mouth, but nothing came out.

Those beautiful blue eyes darkened with concern. Not concern like *I will love and cherish you until the day you die* concern. More like *What mental hospital did you escape from?* concern.

But TJ was determined to say something, anything. Unfortunately, she did: "You're . . . you're gorgeous."

* * * * *

"Blah-blah-blah
blah-blah-blah
blah-blah-blah"

At least that's what Chad heard over his cell phone as Hesper, his sorta girlfriend, kept talking and talking and talking some more. Honestly, did the girl ever stop to take a breath?

But Chad was a nice guy and didn't want to be rude, so he let her continue

"Blah-blah-blah
blah-blah-blah
blah-blah-blah"-ing

Of course, it would help if the *blah*-ing wasn't always about Hesper. Then again, it wasn't her fault that she had her own TV series on the Dizzy Channel. It wasn't her fault everyone made a fuss over her. And it wasn't her fault she thought the world revolved around her. (Actually, not the world; more like the entire solar system or galaxy or . . . well, you get the idea.)

The only good thing about her talking so much was that it drowned out his parents' fighting. It was like a rule or something. Whenever Dad visited, Chad's parents fought. Even though they'd been divorced for, like, forever, you could always plan on the world's biggest shouting match whenever he stopped by. Funny how people think having money makes you happy. As far as Chad figured, it was just the opposite.

Anyway, now he was sitting at his desk, slaving over a book report. Well, if you call staring out your second-story window at the house next door and thinking about your new neighbor "slaving." He guessed her window was the closest to his. And I do mean *close*. Houses on the beach were built so tightly together that if you sneezed, your neighbor could reach out the window and hand you a tissue.

But her window was closed and her lights were out. She was probably already in bed. And who could blame her? It must have been a busy day for her. Busy and embarrassing . . .

First there was the crashing of his party—as in **CRASHING.**

Then there was making the big splash—as in **BIG SPLASH.**

Finally, when he pulled her out of the pool, all she could do was stand around shivering and stuttering. And trying to fix her hair. Lots of trying to fix her hair.

Girls. Go figure.

Once they'd taken her inside and she dried off, he had tried to help her relax by saying he'd see her in school tomorrow. She smiled, tried fixing her hair, and ran out the door.

(Well, she meant to run out the door. There was that little problem of forgetting to open it first.)

The best Chad figured, she had some mental issues. He'd never met a mentally challenged person before, but it was cool. If she needed his help, he'd be there to lend a hand.

In the meantime, there was his book report and, of course . . .

"Blah-blah-blah blah-blah-blah blah-blah-blah"

Hesper.

* * * * *

"TJ?" Little Dorie whispered into her big sister's face. "TJ, you awake?"

"No," TJ said, "I'm sound asleep."

"TJ?"

"Don't bother me."

"TJ, wake up."

Trying to ignore Dorie was like trying to figure out compound fractions: impossible. Her cute little fingers began prying open TJ's unhappy little eyelids. And a moment later, TJ was staring at her sister's blurry face two inches in front of her.

Knowing the routine, TJ pulled back the covers and said, "All right, get in, Squid."

Dorie crawled into the bed and scooted her back nice and close to TJ. Ever since Mom died, Dorie had a hard time sleeping by herself. And although

TJ pretend to be annoyed by her (pretending to be annoyed is Rule #1 in the *Big Sister Handbook*), she understood.

Funny, it had been almost a year, but it felt like yesterday. People always said it would get better, but TJ had her doubts. It's like there was this big hole inside her chest that would never, *never*, go away. Dorie and Vi felt it too. And so did Dad.

In fact, though she would never tell anybody, one time she caught him down in the kitchen late at night. She stood there, unseen in the shadows, and watched him shuffling around, warming some milk in a pan . . . and crying. She'd never seen her dad cry before. And it broke her heart. Even now, when she thought about it, it made the back of her throat ache.

They never talked much about Mom's death. In fact, one of the reasons the family moved here from Missouri was to make a fresh start. But every once in a while, like when they heard the word *cancer*, you could see them get a little teary-eyed. That's why TJ didn't mind Dorie's nightly visits . . . no matter how freezing cold her little feet were.

"You scared?" Dorie whispered.

"About what?" TJ asked.

"Starting a new school tomorrow."

"Nah," TJ lied.

"Me, too," Dorie said.

TJ pretended to yawn. "I met half the kids from school over at Chad's this afternoon. They already know what a klutz I am, so the hard part's over."

Dorie giggled. "You like him, don't you?"

"Who?"

"Chad."

"Good night, Squid."

"You do."

"Good night."

She snuggled closer, shoving those ice cube feet against TJ's legs. TJ was about to complain when Dorie's whole body stiffened. "What's that?" she asked.

TJ tried to ignore her. But as always, ignoring Dorie was impossible.

"Listen," she said. "Someone's whispering."

"It's just the ocean," TJ mumbled. "You'll get used to it."

"TJ?" Dorie squirmed around to face her. Her garlic-with-extra-onion breath told TJ she hadn't brushed her teeth since this afternoon's pizza.

Once again Dorie's hand was on TJ's face, feeling for her eyes. TJ saved her the trouble and opened them. Well, at least one of them. With the other she gave her world-famous *annoyed big sister* squint.

"Listen," Dorie said.

TJ squinted harder. But then she heard it too.

"Return to the pod," a voice whispered.

"I just wanna make sure she's safe, dude," a second voice answered.

TJ bolted up in bed.

"You simply wish to spy on her," the first voice said.

"Do not."

"Do too."

"Do not."

TJ turned to Dorie, whose eyes were as big as Frisbees. She reached for her glasses on the nightstand, slipped them on, and scanned the room, trying to see into the darkness. As the oldest, TJ had talked Dad into letting her have her own bedroom. Which was extremely cool . . . well, except for the part about its being haunted!

TJ swallowed. "Who's . . . ?" Her voice squeaked like a rusty hinge. She tried again. "Who's there?"

"Oh, man, now you torked it."

"How can she possibly hear us?"

Dorie scooted closer. TJ barely noticed her ice feet. It's hard noticing ice feet when you're shivering in frozen fear.

"She can't see us, can she?"

"How should I know?"

TJ took a shaky breath and shouted again. "Who's there?"

"*Don't answer her.*"

"*What type of fool do you think I am?*"

"*How many types are there?*"

"*Ho, ho, you're a real comedian, dude.*"

For ghosts, they didn't exactly sound like the scary type. TJ tried again. "Who's there?!"

No answer.

"Hello?"

Repeat in the no-answer department.

TJ strained to hear even the slightest sound, the slightest breathing, the slightest anything. She stared at the unopened boxes in the middle of her room.

Nothing.

She tried one last time. Lowering her voice so she sounded in charge, she bellowed, "Is anyone there?!"

And then, ever so faintly, she heard the answer:

"*No.*"

CHAPTER TWO

New Friends
(and Enemies)

TIME TRAVEL LOG:

Malibu, California, October 10

Begin Transmission:

Accidental contact with subject. Thanks to our superior intelligence, she suspects nothing. Will follow to school for further observation. Time pod still out of fuel. Tuna is sure he can find some. I'm sure we're in deep quod-quod.

End Transmission.

It was tough going back to sleep. Knowing your room is haunted by ghosts (even if they have low

IQs) can do that to a person. Luckily, there were no more voices. TJ guessed even ghosts needed their beauty sleep. She was also glad she didn't have any weird and scary dreams.

No, the nightmares didn't start till the following morning, her first day at Malibu Junior High. . . .

For starters, why would anybody torture kids by making them take PE (better known as *P*hysical *E*mbarrassment) first thing in the morning? Not that there's anything wrong with freezing to death as you run around the track. But TJ would have preferred for there to be enough daylight to *see* the track.

To be honest, that really wasn't the problem, since her Midwest-winter legs were so incredibly non-tanned, they lit up the field.

"I can't see where I'm going," one of her bronzed California classmates shouted in the dark.

"Don't worry!" another yelled. "Just follow the new kid with the glow-in-the-dark legs!"

Unfortunately, it wasn't just their tans (or TJ's lack of one) that set her apart from the others. There was also their incredible bodies (and her incredible lack of one). Seriously, TJ felt like she was in the middle of a beauty pageant just going to school there! It's not like they treated her badly or anything. They'd have to act like she existed to do that. And as far as she could tell, other than her night-light legs, she was completely invisible to them—like some homeless person that everyone pretended not to see.

There was one exception. One embarrassing exception . . .

Naomi Simpletwirp.

It's not that Naomi was tall and gangly and an AV geek. It's just that . . . well, all right, she *was* tall and gangly and an AV geek. And if you were trying to make a good impression on your first day of school, she was definitely *not* someone you wanted to be hanging with. TJ felt bad for being so judgmental, but hey, she didn't invent the rules. It's not her fault she was feeling what she felt, because she was feeling what she felt when she was feeling it.

TRANSLATION: *Oh, well.*

But no matter how hard she tried to ditch Naomi, it was like the girl was permanently glued to her side, a self-appointed tour guide.

They'd met during the second half of PE, when they were playing dodgeball. The game had barely started before TJ was overcome with the smell of spearmint and the deafening sound of someone

click-ing, *clack*-ing,

and

crunch-ing

way too many breath mints.

Naomi had a thing about breath mints. She also had a thing about deodorants, bath oils, perfumes, odor-eater foot pads, and anything else she thought would make her smell beautiful. (I guess you could say she hadn't quite grasped the concept of *inner* beauty yet.)

Her very first words to TJ were a warning: "Whatever you do, don't hit Hesper."

TJ looked at her. "Who?"

Naomi motioned to a gorgeous blonde on the other team who looked like one of those famous TV stars. The reason was simple. She *was* one of those famous TV stars. And if you couldn't tell it by her perfect hair and perfect beauty, you could tell by the way all the other girls made such a big deal over her.

"Hesper, please throw my ball."
"Hesper, please let the ball hit me."
"Hesper, please let me go out for you."

TJ blinked. "Is that Hesper Breakahart?"

Naomi nodded. "She goes to school here when she isn't filming."

TJ turned back and watched in amazement. Hesper was even prettier than on TV—though that might have been because of the hairstylist and makeup people standing on the sidelines.

One of her smaller groupies ran toward her with a ball. "Here, Hesper, I caught this one just for you."

"Why, thank you, uh . . . What's your name again?"

"I'm Elizabeth, your best friend since forever."

"Oh, that's right. Well, thank you . . ."

"Elizabeth," her best friend since forever said.

Hesper smiled. "That's right." Then, taking the ball, she tossed back her thick mane of hair and after a gleaming white smile, hurled the ball with all of her might. But having superslim arms doesn't exactly make you strong. Which explains why the ball floated through the air like a feather and gently dropped into TJ's hands for an easy catch.

But instead of congratulating TJ, Naomi shouted, "What are you doing?"

TJ looked at her. "What?"

"Hesper threw that!"

"So?"

"So drop it!"

"What?"

Without explaining, Naomi knocked the ball out of her hand.

"Why did you do that?" TJ demanded.

"You're out."

"I'm *out*?"

"Yippee!" Hesper squealed, clapping her hands and jumping up and down. "She's out! She's out! She's out!"

Which meant the rest of her team had no choice but to squeal, clap their hands, jump up and down, and shout, "She's out! She's out! She's out!"

TJ turned to their teacher, Coach Steroidson. "That's not fair."

Coach Steroidson blew her whistle and, being the fair adult she was, shouted, "Finkelstein, you're out!"

TJ just stared at her, then turned and stared at Naomi.

"Trust me," Naomi said in a nervous whisper. "It's for your own good. No one ever beats Hesper at anything."

Another girl fired another ball. TJ caught it, but it didn't make any difference since she was already out. Unfortunately, what *did* make a difference was the *third* ball someone threw. The ball that bounced off the one TJ was holding. The ball that went sailing high into the air and suddenly did a very strange U-turn, before flying directly at Hesper.

"Hesper!" Coach Steroidson shouted. "Look out!"

Tossing back her hair and flashing those pearly whites, she said, "What—?"

She would have said more, but it's hard talking when a ball smashes into your face at a hundred miles per hour.

It's hard talking, but it's not hard screaming.

"My nose!" Her hands flew to her face. "You broke my nose! YOU BROKE MY NOSE!"

Everyone gathered around her, cooing, crying, and showing their concern . . . well, except for those gathered around TJ, who were growling, hissing, and showing their hatred.

Not exactly the good first impression TJ was hoping for. But the day was young, and she would have more opportunities. . . . Unfortunately, she would have plenty more.

* * * * *

Chad stood with a handful of other students in the parking lot as they carried Hesper to the ambulance. (Apparently her stretch limo wasn't handy.) They could have loaded her into a regular car, but what type of drama would that be? And as Chad well knew, the drama queen loved her drama.

In fact, even as they closed the ambulance doors, he could hear her trying for an Academy Award:

"Oh, my nose (*sob, sob*). I'll never be able to smell again!"

"Oh, my nose (*cry, cry*). I'll never be able to act again!"

"Oh, my nose (*wail, wail*). Did someone call *Entertainment Tonight* so I can make this evening's segment?"

Good ol' Hesper.

The only things worse than her drama were the rumors being spread by her so-called friends (spelled f-a-n-s). The rumors that kept growing and growing . . .

"Hey, Chad, did you hear about the new girl beating up Hesper?"

"Hey, Chad, did you hear about the new girl breaking all of Hesper's bones?"

"Hey, Chad, did you hear about the new girl stealing an Army tank and running over Hesper . . . twice?"

Of course he felt bad for Hesper. After all, he was her boyfriend (at least according to Hesper). But he felt even worse for the new kid. Not only did she have her mental issues, but now she was hated by the entire school.

* * * * *

"TJ!" Naomi banged on the stall in the girls' bathroom. "Come on out!"

But TJ was in no mood for coming out. Actually, at the moment, she wasn't so keen on living.

"How could the dodgeball do that?" she moaned. "Make a major U-turn in the air like that? That's impossible!"

More banging from Naomi. "Come on, you can't stay in there forever."

TJ glanced around at the beige steel walls. "Why

not? Hang a few posters, put up a bookshelf, bring in my stereo. The place has potential."

"It gets no sunlight," Naomi argued.

TJ frowned. "What's that got to do with anything?"

"Without the sun, you can never achieve the healthy, golden glow of a Greek goddess."

"I'm going more for the creamy-white look of an Elmer's glue bottle."

"How would you work out?"

"Work out?"

"You know, burn off those empty carbs, trim those flabby thighs, tighten that tummy?"

"Naomi, is that all you ever think—?"

"And where would you get the facial cream to give your skin that young, vibrant look that boys find so attrac—?"

"Naomi—"

"—or teeth-whitening strips for that dazzling smile every girl—?"

"All right, all right." TJ unlocked the stall door and pushed it open to see Naomi. The girl had moved to the mirror and started flossing her teeth.

"You happy now?" TJ sighed.

"Not till we get you to your next class."

"But everyone hates me."

Naomi turned and walked toward her. "Don't be ridiculous. Only the kids in PE hate you."

"Isn't that enough?"

She slipped her arm through TJ's and they started toward the door. "Not when there's a whole school out there waiting to join them. Come on."

Of course, TJ wasn't crazy about everyone seeing her and Naomi together. But since Naomi was like the only human being on the planet who would still talk to her, she didn't have much choice.

Exactly 2 minutes and 17 seconds later, TJ stood in front of Mr. Beaker's science class, under the gaze of 28 pairs of freezing eyes. Actually, only 27 because Chad Steel was there. And his warm baby blues weren't exactly freezing her out . . . more like melting her down.

(Insert dreamy *sigh* here.)

"Class," Mr. Beaker said, "this is Thelma Jean Finkelstein. She's a transfer student from Mississippi, and I want you to make her feel right at home."

"Actually—" TJ cleared her throat—"that's Missouri."

"Pardon me?"

"I'm from Missouri."

"Mississippi, Missouri—" he waved his hand— "They're all the same."

She could think of a few million people who might disagree, but since he taught science and not geography, she let it go.

He picked up a clipboard and continued. "Everyone's been working on their science fair projects with their lab partners. But since everyone has a partner, I'm afraid—"

"Mr. Beaker?" a little voice squeaked.

He came to a stop and looked at a geeky kid who had a drippy faucet for a nose and 0 percent fashion sense.

"Yes, Doug?"

The kid pushed up his glasses. "I don't have a partner."

Mr. Beaker glanced down at his clipboard. "Hmm . . ."

Doug sniffed loudly. He looked at TJ longingly, then gave an even louder sniff followed by an even longinglier look. (Okay, maybe *longinglier* isn't a word, but it should be by the way he was staring.)

Then, just when it seemed like TJ's life was going to be ruined twice in the same day, another voice chimed in from the back of the room. "Me neither."

She glanced over to see Chad Steel.

Mr. Beaker looked up. "You don't have a partner, Mr. Steel?"

Chad shook his head.

Elizabeth (Hesper Breakahart's best friend since forever) pointed at TJ. "Not since that witch broke her nose this morning."

Hesper Breakahart? TJ thought. *Hesper Breakahart was Chad Steel's lab partner? Oh, brother . . .*

"Hmm . . ." Mr. Beaker looked back down at his clipboard. "So we have two choices, do we? Hmm . . ." And then, to heighten the suspense, he threw in another "Hmm . . ." for good measure.

TJ caught her breath. Was it possible? Could Chad really become her lab partner? She crossed her fingers, wishing with all her might it would be true.

She threw a look over to Doug, who gave another sniff and another look . . . topped off by a good wipe of the nose on the back of his hand. She crossed her arms, her ankles, and her eyes—not exactly her best look, but she'd do anything to help the odds.

Finally Mr. Beaker glanced up and said, "Well, Ms. Finkelstein, I'll let *you* decide."

"Me?" she croaked.

He nodded. "Do you want Doug Claudlooper as your lab partner or Chad Steel?"

Yes!

She couldn't believe her luck!

Yes! Yes!

She couldn't believe how quickly things had turned around!

Yes! Yes! Yes!

She couldn't believe how Naomi kept waving her arms from the side of the room and mouthing the words *"Not Chad! Not Chad! Not Chad!"*

"Well?" Mr. Beaker asked.

Now, before you think TJ is totally superficial or anything like that, it's important to know that she was sure Doug was a very nice boy. It's not his fault he was wearing Goodwill rejects and binocular glasses and had a perpetual case of hay fever (though someone might want to give him a clue about using tissues instead of the backs of hands).

But we are talking Chad Steel. Who was she to question fate? There was also the fact that they were next-door neighbors, so he could come over and work on the project anytime he wanted . . . and look at her with those baby blues . . . and accidentally brush his hand against hers, then hold it, then reach his lips toward her cheek and—

"Ms. Finkelstein?"

She blinked, coming back to reality.

Mr. Beaker repeated, "Who would you prefer to work with?"

TJ scrunched her face into a frown, pretending to think while doing her best to ignore Naomi, who was still waving her arms and mouthing, *"Not Chad! Not Chad! Not Chad!"*

Finally she nodded toward Chad. "I guess . . . him."

Chad gave a smile and the room started buzzing. Not *happy little bumblebee* buzzing. No, this was more like *swarm of killer bees* buzzing. Everyone was shocked and angry at TJ. Well, everyone but Naomi, who had dropped her head into her hands and was sadly shaking it.

"Then, please—" Mr. Beaker motioned TJ toward the empty desk next to Chad's—"take a seat and join him."

She started forward, floating toward him as in a dream . . . until she was awakened by someone sticking out a foot to trip her.

Actually, she wasn't entirely surprised. With her growing popularity, she didn't plan on running for class president anytime soon. What did surprise her was that when she stumbled and started to fall, Chad leaped to his feet and caught her just before she hit the ground.

It was a beautiful moment. One she would

remember all her life—Chad Steel holding her in his arms and the entire class watching with envy (except for Naomi, who was busy praying). Of course, it would have been more beautiful if a dictionary hadn't suddenly flown off the bookshelf at the side of the room, shot over everyone's desks, and slammed into the back of Chad's head.

What?!

It didn't hurt him or anything, but it definitely got his attention. And everyone else's.

CHAPTER THREE

"Aghhhh . . ."

TIME TRAVEL LOG:

Malibu, California, October 10–supplemental

Begin Transmission:
Have assisted subject through first day of school.
For some reason, she's not grateful. Still unable to
find time pod fuel. Other equipment fritzing from
exposure to saltwater. Majorly questioning Tuna's
engineering skills.

End Transmission

Ever since their mom died, Dorie, Violet, and TJ
made the meals. Dad used to, but after eight weeks

of hot dogs, cold cereal, hot dogs, mac and cheese, and hot dogs, the girls decided to take turns cooking. Well, Dorie and TJ took turns cooking (if you call throwing a frozen dinner in the microwave cooking).

But TJ's middle sister, Vi, did things a little differently.

Since Vi was a vegetarian, health-food fanatic, and all-around germ freak, the family was lucky to get anything that didn't taste like boiled cardboard topped with sawdust sprinkles. For dessert it was usually overcooked water (as long as it was prepared in hypoallergenic pans that had never been exposed to animal by-products).

"So how was everybody's day?" Dad asked cheerfully. Even on his bad days he tried to be cheerful— another reason the girls loved him so.

Their answers were pretty much what you'd expect.

Dorie went on and on, and then on some more, about a ladybug she found on the windowsill of her kindergarten classroom. (Good ol' Dorie. Give her a paper clip to play with and she'd be content for weeks.)

Violet talked about how she'd been elected class secretary, become chess club president, and scored 110 percent on her first math quiz.

And TJ? Well, she dropped into the safe and secure Fine mode. It makes no difference what you're asked; nothing is safer than answering with the tried and true "Fine."

"And, TJ, how was your day?"

"Fine."

"How are you fitting in?"

"Fine."

"How are your teachers?"

"Fine."

Yes, sir, nothing beats the Fine mode . . . especially when you don't exactly feel like shouting, ***"IT WAS TERRIBLE! THE WORST DAY OF MY LIFE! AND I THINK I'M LOSING MY MIND!"***

But Dorie knew something was up. She probably figured TJ was still nervous about last night's voices. (And TJ would have been, if it wasn't for the rest of the day's migraine makers.)

So, trying to help, little Dorie asked, "Dad? Are there such things as ghosts?"

"Why do you ask, sweetheart?"

TJ threw her a *don't you dare go there* look.

Dorie caught it and answered, "Oh, I don't know. I was just wondering if rooms and stuff can be haunted."

"No, sweetheart," he said. "There are no such

things as ghosts. Vi, would you pass me the pencil shavings? They're exceptionally tasty this evening."

TJ sighed quietly in relief. Dad had enough on his mind. He didn't need to worry about haunted rooms. Besides, TJ doubted it was her room that was haunted. After all that happened in school today, she was beginning to wonder if *she* was haunted.

Unfortunately, she was about to find out.

* * * * *

"Blah-blah-blah
blah-blah-blah
blah-blah-blah"

That's right, Chad was back in his room pretending to listen to his girlfriend (while secretly wishing the new kid had broken Hesper's phone instead of her nose).

For about the hundredth time, he rubbed the back of his head, wondering about his own accident in Mr. Beaker's class. Luckily, he wasn't hurt. (If you count getting knocked unconscious by a flying dictionary as *un*hurt.)

And when he came to and looked up, there was the new kid kneeling beside him.

"What happened?" he asked her.

But looking into his eyes, all she could do was answer, "I . . . uh . . . er . . . um . . ." And when she got tired of that, she tried another approach: "Um . . . er . . . uh . . . I . . ."

Poor thing—she really did have some mental issues.

He didn't know which was worse, a girl who never stopped

"Blah-blah-blah blah-blah-blah"-ing

or a girl who didn't know how to start.

Anyway, he was at his desk in his room, once again bruising his brain over that same book report, when a silvery reflection caught his attention. It came from inside the new kid's house. At first he thought it was a mirror or something. Until he realized that

mirrors or somethings don't usually look like . . .
two guys in silver suits crawling out of a large,
glowing egg.

TWO GUYS IN SILVER SUITS CRAWLING OUT OF A LARGE, GLOWING EGG!

(That's for any readers who forgot their glasses.)

Immediately, Chad turned and shouted into his
phone. "Hesper! *Hesper!*"

But of course Hesper was too busy talking to hear.

Now, the way Chad figured, he had three
options:

OPTION #1: Explain to Hesper that he had to
hang up and go save his neighbor's life.

OPTION #2: Hang up without explaining and
go save his neighbor's life.

OPTION #3: Leave the phone open and go
save his neighbor's life.

Since Hesper really didn't need him present to
carry on a conversation, he chose Option #3. He left
the phone on his desk and raced out of the room as
Hesper continued to

"Blah-blah-blah
blah-blah-blah
blah-blah-blah"

* * * * *

Meanwhile, TJ trudged up the stairs to start the evening's torture (better known as homework). Vi was on Dad's computer figuring out the cure for world hunger, and Dorie was helping Dad with the dishes. That just left TJ and the two teenage aliens wearing space suits who were standing in the middle of the hallway.

TWO TEENAGE ALIENS WEARING SPACE SUITS!

(That's for the same forgetful readers).

Great, TJ thought. *Space invaders; that's all I need.*

"Shh," the taller one said to his partner. He was a surfer type with long blonde bangs hanging in his eyes. He sounded like he was right out of the seventies. "Here she comes, dude."

"Quickly," the shorter, chunkier one replied. He

had short red hair and sounded kind of snooty. "Remove the pod before she borks into it."

By now TJ had frozen in her tracks. She wanted to scream and run away, but she had this thing about getting zapped in the back by photon guns or whatever they're killing earthlings with these days. Instead, she watched in terror as they pushed a giant silver egg (the perfect size for two aliens visiting planets) down the hall.

"What is she staring at?" Chunky Guy whispered. "She cannot possibly see us, can she?"

"Quick!" Tall Dude whispered. "Hide!"

They raced to the nearest wall, pressed their faces against it, and covered their eyes.

TJ just kept standing and staring in disbelief.

"What's she doing?" Tall Dude whispered.

Chunky Guy sneaked a peek. "She is standing and staring in disbelief."

"Maybe she actually *does* see us," Tall Dude repeated.

"Don't be toyped; we're invisible."

"Who you calling toyped? You're the one who's toyped!"

"I certainly am not."

"Are too!"

"Well then you're toyped times the square root of pi."

"Yeah, well you're—"

TJ knew it was rude to interrupt, especially with out-of-town (or out-of-galaxy) guests. But she figured it was time to speak up. So, opening her mouth, she shared a brave and very courageous

"AGHH ..."

This must have frightened Tall Dude because he answered with an equally brave and courageous

"AGHH ..."

"What is she screaming at?!" Chunky Guy cried.

"Aliens!" TJ screamed. "I see aliens!"

"Where?!" Tall Dude shouted, looking around in fear.

"AGHHHHHH ...,"

TJ screamed.

"AGHHHHHₕ . . .,"

Tall Dude screamed.

And not wanting to be left out, Chunky Guy joined in the chorus:

"AGHHHHHHHHHHHHHHHH . . ."

"TJ?" Dad called from the bottom of the stairs. "TJ, what's wrong? Are you all right?"

"Quickly," Chunky Guy shouted, "the morphing device!"

"Got it!" Tall Dude cried. He pulled out a large, red object that looked like a Swiss Army Knife and immediately dropped it.

"Oh, brother," Chunky Guy sighed. "Open the Morphing Blade; open the Morphing Blade!"

"TJ?" Dad started up the stairs.

Tall Dude picked up the knife, opened a special blade, and

krinkle . . . krackle
POOF!

turned himself into Abraham Lincoln (complete with that cool hat, though the beard looked a little fake).

"No," Chunky Guy cried, "morph into her; morph into her!"

"I'm trying, dude!" He opened another blade and

krinkle . . . krackle
POOF!

turned himself into the Tin Man from *The Wizard of Oz*.

"No, no, no!" Chunky Guy yelled.

"It's shorting out!" Tall Dude cried. He tried again and

POOF!

turned himself into the Beatles. All four of them! They were just getting ready to play "Yellow Submarine" when suddenly

POOF!

TJ was standing in front of herself. Well, at least someone who looked an awful lot like TJ was standing in front of herself.

"TJ?" Dad was halfway up the steps, almost in sight.

"And her!" Chunky Guy shouted. "Morph her! Morph her!"

The fake TJ opened another blade, and

POOF!

the real TJ was turned into (hang on, this is going to get weird) . . . a floor lamp.

(Hey, I warned you.)

Of course, she wanted to scream, *"A floor lamp?! What am I doing as a floor lamp?!"* But she couldn't. Apparently floor lamps don't have mouths to scream with. (They do, however, have very attractive shades with cute little tassels along the bottom, not to mention nifty three-way switches.)

Meanwhile, Chunky Guy raced to the giant floating egg, pushed it through the nearby bathroom door, and hid with it out of sight . . . just as Dad arrived.

"TJ?" Dad asked the fake TJ. "What's all the screaming about?"

"I'm sorry," Fake TJ said in a high-pitched voice. "I was just practicing for the talent show."

"Talent show?" Dad asked.

"Yes, I'm trying out."

"Well, that's great. I'm glad you're working to fit in."

"Thanks," Fake TJ said, his voice cracking slightly.

Dad tilted his head. "Are you okay? You sound strange."

"Oh, that." Fake TJ coughed slightly. "I might be coming down with a cold."

"Well, go to bed early tonight," Dad said. "I don't want you getting sick before your big audition."

"Good idea. Thanks."

He gave a nod and headed back down the steps. Only then did he notice the real TJ (who was now a floor lamp standing next to the wall). "Where'd you get that lamp?"

"Oh, that." Fake TJ pretended to giggle. "I found it in my closet. Can I keep it?"

He scowled. "I don't know. It's pretty ugly."

Hey, Real TJ thought, *even us floor lamps have feelings!*

"Please?" Fake TJ begged. "I know just the place for it."

Dad hesitated, then shrugged. "Sure, it's your room. Why not?"

"Great." Fake TJ beamed.

Dad nodded and headed for the stairs. "I love you, TJ."

"I love you too, Poppsy," Fake TJ said.

Poppsy? Real TJ thought. *What person on earth calls their dad Poppsy?* (Then she remembered Fake TJ wasn't exactly a person from earth.)

Dad shook his head in amusement and continued down the steps.

As soon as the coast was clear, Fake TJ pulled out another blade from his Swiss Army Knife and

krinkle ...krackle
POOF!

morphed back into his tall, surfer self.

"That was close," Chunky Guy said as he came back into the room.

"Fur sure," Tall Dude agreed. Then, turning to the floor lamp, he said, "I don't know how you can see us. Must be something majorly zworked with our cloaking device. But if we turn you back into you, do you promise not to scream again?"

TJ tried to answer but ran into the same *I can't talk without a mouth* problem.

Chunky Guy rolled his eyes. "She is not capable of answering us."

"Oh, right," Tall Dude said. "I knew that." He turned to TJ. "Okay, then, blink once for yes and twice for no."

TJ tried to nod, but without a head, nodding can also be a little difficult. So, concentrating with all her might,

grrrr, errrr, arrrr,

she imagined turning on her lightbulb. And sure enough, after a few more *grrrr*s, *errrr*s, and *arrrr*s, it came on! But only for a second before it went off.

"Great." Chunky Guy smiled.

TJ was so impressed with herself that she did it again.

"That's two times," Tall Dude said. "So you *are* going to scream?"

No, no, no, TJ thought. She blinked the light a third time. Then a fourth.

"What's she doing?" Tall Dude asked.

"As you may recall, the history holographs say her math skills are somewhat limited."

"Oh yeah."

"Let us proceed to the room," Chunky Guy said. "Perhaps if we sit down and explain everything, she will cooperate."

Tall Dude nodded and walked toward her.

Of course TJ blinked again and again, hoping Dad or Violet or little Dorie would hear—er, see her. Unfortunately, no one did. No one except the two aliens who she was about to discover weren't really aliens at all.

CHAPTER FOUR

Blink, Blink, Blink, Blink, Blink, Blink, Blink, Blink

TIME TRAVEL LOG:

Malibu, California, October 10—supplemental

Begin Transmission:
Cloaking device has failed. Subject sees and hears
us. Must now brief her on project . . . while trying
not to flush her next-door neighbor down the toilet.

End Transmission

Tall Dude picked TJ up and carried her into her
room, where she listened carefully. Well, as carefully
as a floor lamp with fancy trim around the shade
can listen.

"Allow me to introduce myself," Chunky Guy said. "My name is Thomas Uriah Norman Alphonso . . . the third."

"We call him Tuna, for short," Tall Dude said as he pushed the floating egg through the doorway and into the room.

Tuna nodded toward Tall Dude. "And we call him Herby, which, unfortunately, is short for—"

"Herby," Herby said, flipping his blond bangs out of his eyes.

TJ blinked her light off and on.

"What's she saying?" Herby asked.

"Do I look like I speak lamp-ese?" Tuna said.

"Hang on, Your Dude-ness," Herby said. "Let me get out the translator."

Once again he pulled out his Swiss Army Knife and opened another blade. And once again he fumbled it, dropping it to the floor. Only this time, instead of people turning into presidents or famous rock-and-roll bands, TJ heard:

"Hm, this is interesting; can I eat it? Hm, a nice shiny blade; can I eat it? Hm, a nice red handle; can I eat it? Hm, a nice—"

Then she saw the cockroach scurrying up and over the knife.

Great! she thought. *Not only is my place infested by space aliens, I've got cockroaches, too!*

"Zweegs," Tuna cringed.

"Zweegs to the max," Herby agreed. He raised his foot over the insect as the translator continued to translate:

"Hm, a nice foot up there; can I eat it? Hm, a nice shoe coming down toward me; can I eat it? Hm, a nice–"

SPLAT!

Zweegs.

Tuna and Herby both shuddered.

Blink-blink, blink-blink, TJ blinked.

"All right." Herby, the surfer dude, turned to TJ. "I'm not sure why you can see us. I'm guessing my partner here hasn't totally fixed the cloaking device."

"Or," Tuna argued, "*my* partner doesn't know the first thing about using it."

"I'd know how to use it if you knew how to fix it."

"Oh yeah?"

"Yeah!"
"Yeah?"
"Yeah!"

TJ looked on in amazement. It was hard knowing which boy had fewer brain cells. But since you can't get much lower than one, she figured it was a tie. To get their attention, she started

blink, **blink**, blink

blink, blink, blink-ing

again.

Tuna was the first to spot her. Straightening his suit, he cleared his throat and started over. "First of all, despite our appearance, we are not spacemen."

"Or bodybuilders," Herby said, sucking in his stomach and sticking out his chest, "which some folks mistake us for."

Tuna gave him a look, then continued. "Actually, we are time travelers."

"From the 23rd century," Herby added.

"And we have traveled back through time to observe you for our history project."

Blink-blink? TJ blinked.

"That's right." Herby nodded. "*You*. And not just 'cause we think you're, like, a major babe. OWW!"

(The "OWW!" came after Tuna stomped on his foot.)

As Herby was busy hopping up and down on one foot, Tuna calmly continued. "We have returned to your time because when you grow up, you will become a great world leader. In fact, one day you will—"

"TJ?" Dad suddenly called from downstairs. "You've got company."

TJ *blink-blink*ed in concern.

"What do we do?" Herby cried.

"How should I know?"

"Hey, dude, you got us into this quod-quod!"

"Why must you always blame me?"

"Because you're always wrong."

"Am not."

"Are too."

"Am—"

"TJ?" Dad called from the bottom of the stairs.

TJ *blink-blink, blink-blink*ed faster.

Tuna frowned. "Permit me a moment to think."

"TJ?!"

But Herby had no time for moments (or thinking). He took a deep breath and gave the world's second-worst imitation of TJ. (The first was back on page 43). "Send him on up, Poppsy."

"Send him on up?" Tuna cried. "Are you toyped?!"

"It's better than us going down there," Herby said.

"It is not."

"Is too."

"Is not."

By now TJ was blinking faster than a strobe light after too much sugar and way too many cups of coffee.

Then they all heard the dreaded

knock-knock-**knock**

The boys froze. So did TJ—though she didn't have much choice, being a floor lamp.

knock-knock-**knock**

"Who is it?" Herby asked in his high, TJ voice.

"It's Chad, from next door. Are you all right?"

"Oh no," Tuna groaned.

"Way oh no," Herby moaned.

Blink-blink-blink-blink-blink-blink-blink-blink-blink,
TJ blinked.

"Open the knife," Tuna said as he headed for the door. "Let us Freeze-Frame him."

"Got it," Herby said as he scooped up the knife and followed his partner.

Tuna opened the bedroom door, and there stood Chad in all of his wonderful . . . Chadness.

"Uh, you're not TJ," he said.

"No, I am," Herby said in his TJ voice.

Chad looked over to Herby and scowled. The voice may have been TJ's, but the body sure wasn't.

"Now!" Tuna shouted.

Herby opened the blade, and

krinkle . . . **krackle**
POOF!

Chad was morphed into a goldfish.

"You morphed him?" Tuna yelled. "You were supposed to Freeze Frame him!"

"The blades are all mixed up!" Herby cried.

Both boys (and the floor lamp) looked down at the goldfish flopping on the floor.

"What do we do now?" Herby shouted.

"Place him in water before he dies," Tuna yelled.

"Right!" Herby dropped to his knees and tried to scoop Chad up into his hands. But the little guy was like a greased pig wearing a banana-peel suit covered in ice.

Translation: *He was slippery.*

TJ watched in horror as her next-door neighbor slipped out of Herby's hands, once, twice, three times, before Herby finally caught the little fellow and rose to his feet.

Herby turned to her. "A glass of water? Do you have a glass of water?"

Blink-blink-blink-blink.

"I believe that's a no!" Tuna cried.

"What do we do?" Herby shouted.

"The bathroom! Down the hall!"

Herby nodded and raced out the door.

"But not the sink!" Tuna shouted. "He'll jump out of the sink."

"Then where?" Herby called over his shoulder.

"The toilet bowl!"

"Right!" Herby yelled. "Good thinking!"

"Of course it is!" Tuna agreed. "That's what I do best!"

But apparently TJ didn't agree. Which explains her response:

*Blink-blink-blink-blink-blink-blink-blink-
blink-blink-blink-blink-blink-blink-blink-blink-
blink-blink-blink-blink-blink-blink-blink-
blink-blink-blink-blink-blink-blink-blink-blink-
blink-blink-blink-blink-blink-blink-blink-
blink-blink-blink-blink-blink-blink-blink-blink-
blink-blink . . .*

A minute later, Herby was back.

"Is everything secure?" Tuna asked.

"Cool." Herby nodded. "Chad is swimming his little heart out."

"Excellent." Tuna turned to TJ, who was busy flashing her little bulb out.

"What's with her?" Herby asked.

"Perhaps she is experiencing some sort of electrical malfunction."

Of course, if they would have bothered to ask TJ

what she was saying (and given her a mouth to say it), they might have heard something like:

"YOU PUT CHAD STEEL IN OUR TOILET?! ARE YOU NUTS?! DON'T YOU KNOW THAT WITH THREE GIRLS AND ONE BATHROOM, HE'LL BE FLUSHED AWAY IN 1.2 MINUTES!"

But they didn't know because they didn't ask. And they didn't ask because, as TJ had already figured out, neither one of them was the brightest crayon in the box. Actually, as far as she could tell, they didn't even know what a crayon was.

"Perhaps instead of explaining why we are here," Tuna said, "we should show her."

"Groovy," Herby said as he reached for the Swiss Army Knife.

"Actually—" Tuna cleared his throat—"do you mind if I do the honors?"

"You don't trust me?" Herby asked.

"Should I?"

Herby paused to think, then nodded. "Good point." He tossed the knife to Tuna, who opened another blade.

TJ closed her eyes, fearing the worst.

But this time there were no bug translations and no morphing. Instead, everything was perfectly normal. Well, except for the part where they were

... transported to Washington DC
... watching a future president being sworn in
... who just happened to be a woman
... who just happened to look like an older version of TJ.

Other than that, everything was perfectly normal. (Although being the only flashing lamp in the crowd accompanied by two boys in time-travel suits did raise an eyebrow or two.)

"What you are witnessing," Tuna said, "is a holographic image of the future. It is being projected into your room."

TJ could only stare with amazement.

"Pretty outloopish, huh," Herby said proudly. "And see that lady-type up there being sworn in? She just happens to be you in forty-two years."

TJ blinked in disbelief.

"He is correct," Tuna said. "You, Thelma Jean Finkelstein, will become one of the greatest leaders

in history. You will single-handedly eliminate world
hunger, wipe out major diseases, end poverty, and—"

"Bring back the hula hoop," Herby added.

Tuna gave him a look, then grudgingly admitted,
"And bring back the hula hoop."

"That's why we were so stoked on choosing you
for our history project," Herby said. "That and your
great babe-ness."

(This time he moved his foot so Tuna missed it
when he tried to stomp it.)

Gathering himself together, Tuna continued. "We
wished to discover how you acquired the character
qualities to become such an outstanding leader."

Herby nodded toward Tuna. "Unfortunately,
Mr. Brainiac here forgot to gas up our time-travel
pod, so we're, like, totally stuck here till we can score
some fuel."

Blink.

"Yeah, I know; bummer."

"However, there is one other problem," Tuna said.

"Oh yeah," Herby sighed. "No offense, little Dude-
ness, but right now you got like zero of those character qualities."

Blink-blink?

"You know, all the cool stuff—like honesty, thoughtfulness, self-sacrifice, respect for others— they're, like, totally zworked."

TJ blinked in protest.

"No, it is quite true," Tuna said. "Simply consider the way you're treating Naomi."

"And that Doug dude," Herby added.

TJ frowned—or at least she tried to.

Tuna explained, "The young lady with the AV skills and the self-image problem . . . and the young man in science class with all the allergies?"

TJ sighed. (Well, if she could have sighed, she would have sighed.) It was true; she'd barely given either of them the time of day.

Tuna continued, "And according to our history holographs, one of your greatest traits will be your ability to look past the superficial and see what a person is really like on the inside."

"But right now, you're, like, totally ignoring the little dudes and dudettes, while going gam-gam over the Chad Steels of the world."

Well, of course, TJ thought. *Because Chad Steel is so . . . so . . . IN TROUBLE, SWIMMING INSIDE OUR*

TOILET BOWL! Once again she started blinking furiously.

"What's she saying now?" Tuna asked.

As if to answer his question, Dorie's little voice screamed from the bathroom:

"EWWWWW!"

Tuna and Herby traded looks of alarm.
TJ blinked faster.

"THERE'S A GOLDFISH IN THE TOILET!"

'That was the one thing none of them wanted to hear.

Actually, there was one other thing that was slightly worse. The sound of a toilet being

flushed.

CHAPTER FIVE

Outloopish to the Max

TIME TRAVEL LOG:
Malibu, California, October 10—supplemental
of supplemental

Begin Transmission:
Thanks to incredible reflexes, neighbor boy is
saved. But instead of praise, subject appears
majorly unthrilled. Despite efforts to dazzle her
with good looks, charm, and incredible intelligence,
she remains unimpressed. 21st century girls.
Go figure.

End Transmission

Chad rolled over in bed and looked at his radio alarm.

It read 11:48 p.m.

He shook his head. What a dream. Crazy aliens . . . blinking floor lamps . . . and a few thousand laps around a toilet bowl. Talk about a nightmare.

Of course he'd be more convinced it was only a nightmare if he wasn't still wearing his clothes and shoes.

He'd be even more convinced if they weren't dripping wet.

And he'd be 100 percent convinced if he didn't have what tasted like

smack, **SMACK**, smack

fish food flakes stuck to the roof of his mouth and between his teeth.

He quickly threw off his covers and

squeak-slosh,
squeak-slosh-ed

to the bathroom, where he poured one glass of water to rinse his mouth

spit-tue*ee*

and a second glass to

cough-cough

choke-*choke*

breathe.

(Old habits die hard.)

Anyway, when he realized he no longer had gills, he

**squeak-*slosh*,
squeak-slosh-ed**

back to his room and got into some dry pajamas.

Only then, as he lay in his bed, did he notice that his cell phone was still open on his desk. He didn't exactly see it. More like he

"blah, blah, blah blah, blah, blah"

heard it. That's right, Hesper was still talking away. And as he drifted off to sleep, Chad wondered which would run out of energy first. His cell phone battery or

"blah, blah, blah blah, blah, blah"

Hesper Breakahart.

* * * * *

Actually, it hadn't been too hard for the guys to save Chad. All they had to do was find the right blade to Freeze-Frame time, scoop Chad out of the water, and put him in his bed . . . while everyone else stood around frozen like statues.

(Well, everyone but TJ, since lamps are pretty much like statues anyway.)

It also wasn't hard turning TJ back into a real person. Well, except that the morphing device was still on the fritz.

No problem if you don't mind little inconveniences like first being turned into the

krinkle . . . krackle

POOF!

toenail clipping of a giant elephant (and you thought a fish in the toilet bowl was gross). Or a

krinkle . . . **krackle**

POOF!

half-used tube of toothpaste (squeezed in the middle, of course). And finally a

krinkle . . . krackle

POOF!

humpback whale.

Anyway, once TJ was finally back to normal (except for the handful of barnacles they had to scrape off her back), she'd looked at Tuna and Herby, and in her most gentle voice . . . screamed her lungs out.

"THIS IS NUTS! I DON'T WANT TO BE IN YOUR STUPID HISTORY PROJECT!"

"Shh." Herby motioned for her to be quiet.

"WHAT DO YOU MEAN, SHH?!"

"By yelling, you will awaken your family," Tuna warned.

"I'LL YELL IF I WANT TO YELL!"

"Well, all right, then," Tuna said, pulling out the Swiss Army Knife and opening a new blade.

"NOW WHAT ARE YOU DOING? STOP IT! DON'T YOU DARE POINT THAT THING AT–"

Sizzle . . . *Sizzle*
POP!

"–me. Wait a minute. My voice. What have you done to my voice!?"

"I have simply reduced your volume."

"You can't do that!"

"I'm afraid I have no choice."

"All right, all right, I'll talk softer!"

"Do I have your word?"

"Yes, yes!"

And so, after another

Sizzle ...Sizzle
POP!

TJ returned to her normal volume . . . and the three of them had a very long talk, late into the night.

First of all, TJ made it clear that she was flattered to be somebody's history project, but she was definitely not interested in being "observed."

"Oh, we have very strict rules in the matter," Tuna explained.

"That's right, Your Dude-ness. There's absolutely no gawking at you when you're asleep or changing clothes or—"

"Look, I appreciate that, but you have to understand I'm having a hard enough time just fitting in at school."

"That's why we've been, like, helping," Herby said.

Tuna shot him a look, but it was too late.

"Helping?" TJ asked suspiciously. "What do you mean . . . *helping*?"

"Oh, I don't know," Herby said modestly. "Maybe like making dodgeballs do U-turns in midair."

"That was you?" TJ cried.

"Or sending dictionaries flying across the room to knock out handsome lab partners."

"You did that?!"

"He's really not your type, you know," Tuna said.

"That's right," Herby agreed. "Especially with super-intelligent, good-looking 23rd century dudes like us who just happen to be hanging around."

TJ could only stare at him.

Herby could only grin back (and maybe hold in his stomach a little).

Finally TJ shook her head. "No. Absolutely not." She began pacing the room. "No way. Definitely not."

"Yeah, but—"

"No."

"We could—"

"Forget it."

"But—"

"No way."

After a dozen more *buts* and a hundred more *no ways*, the boys finally gave in.

"Well . . . all right, then," Tuna said sadly. "If that's your final word, we shall depart."

TJ folded her arms. "It's my final word."

Tuna nodded. "Just as soon as we fuel up our time-travel pod, we'll be on our way."

TJ started to relax. "Great. There's a gas station just down the street."

"Actually," Herby corrected, "we don't exactly use gasoline."

"Oh." TJ started to unrelax. "What exactly do you use?"

The boys traded nervous looks.

TJ's unrelaxedness grew even more unrelaxed.

Tuna swallowed and answered, "We will need a nuclear submarine plutonium power pack."

"A nuclear submarine plutonium power pack?!"

"Shh . . . ," Tuna said, reaching for the Swiss Army Knife.

TJ immediately lowered her voice. "Where do you get that?"

"From one of your top-secret nuclear-powered submarines."

"TOP-SECRET NUCLEAR-POWERED SUBMARINES?!"

Tuna opened the Volume Control Blade.

"Okay, okay, sorry," TJ whispered. "But don't you think that might be just a teensy bit difficult?"

"Actually," Herby said, "it will be nearly impossible."

"NEARLY IMPOS—"

sizzle . . . Sizzle

POP!

—sible?" TJ cried.

Tuna answered. "*Nearly* impossible is not the same as *completely* impossible."

"That's right," Herby said. "It's the other thing that's *completely* impossible."

"Other thing?" TJ asked.

"Yeah."

"Which is?" TJ expected the worst.

"Which is like this totally outloopish chili recipe invented by a Texas housewife."

"That's correct," Tuna said. "In 50 years it will be discovered to be the most powerful fuel known to mankind."

"Why is getting a chili recipe so hard?" TJ asked.

Once again the boys traded looks.

"Guys?" TJ repeated. "What's so hard about getting a chili recipe?"

Tuna answered, "Because at the moment that housewife is only two and a half years old."

TJ's heart sank.

"And don't forget the chili, dude," Herby said. "It only works after it's been digested by a flock of ostriches from Africa."

"That goes without saying," Tuna said.

TJ could only shake her head, wishing they hadn't said what they said went without saying when they said it.

TRANSLATION: This was definitely not one of her better days.

CHAPTER SIX

Another Day, Another Catastrophe

TIME TRAVEL LOG:

Malibu, California, October 11

Begin Transmission:
Subject not happy. Waaaay not happy . . .

End Transmission

The good news was Hesper Breakahart did not
return to school the next day and turn all her friends
against TJ.

The bad news was Hesper Breakahart could still
text all those friends. And since all those friends
wanted to be Hesper's *best* friend, that meant TJ
instantly became everyone's *worst* enemy.

It's not that she didn't appreciate the attention, but being Malibu Junior High's public enemy #1 wasn't exactly what she had in mind.

Then there were Tuna and Herby, who stayed glued to her side. They felt responsible to protect her from any and all problems (most likely because they *were* responsible for any and all problems). They'd also fixed the cloaking device, which meant they were once again invisible to everybody . . . well, almost everybody.

"What about me?" TJ whispered as she trudged up the stairs to her locker on the third floor. (Of course all of her classes were on the first floor, so it only made sense to put her locker on the third floor. We'll get to another fact about third floors in just a minute.) "Why am I the only one who can see you?" she asked.

"An excellent question," Tuna whispered back as he floated beside her. "One to which we have no answer."

"Guess you're just lucky," Herby said, catching his reflection in the window and sucking in his gut. The guy was obviously still trying to impress her . . . and he was obviously still failing. Miserably.

"Shouldn't you boys be out looking for your nuclear submarine whatever?" she asked.

"Actually," Tuna replied, "you are our first priority."

"Lucky me," she sighed.

"Exactly. " Herby beamed. He was pleased she was finally getting the point. "You're just lucky."

"Look, fellas," she said, "I don't want you interfering like you did yesterday."

"You mean *helping* like we did yesterday," Herby corrected.

"No, I mean *interfering*."

"Actually, we were looking out for your welfare," Tuna said.

"Actually, busting Hesper's nose only made my life miserable."

"What about the flying dictionary?" Herby argued. "That was pretty good."

"Guys, I'm serious."

"But, Your Dude-ness—"

"No more!" A couple of students glanced at her, and she lowered her voice. "Whatever happens, I'm on my own; understand?"

There was no answer.

"Understand?"

"Understood," Tuna answered gloomily.

"Ditto," Herby sighed.

TJ glanced around and noticed several kids

snickering. "What's going on?" she asked. "Why's everybody laughing?"

Tuna replied, "Perhaps they are not used to girls walking up stairs having lengthy conversations with themselves."

TJ could only shake her head. Now *everyone* thought she was a nutcase.

Everyone but good ol' Naomi

click, clack, crunch

Simpletwirp. Suddenly she and her breath mints pulled up beside TJ.

"Oh, great," TJ muttered. "What else can go wrong?" Of course she remembered the lecture the boys had given her the night before, but come on, this was Naomi Simpletwirp—the geekiest girl in school.

And at least this morning, one of the most talkative.

"So did you hear that Hesper is not coming to school today?" she asked, pulling out some breath spray and taking a hit.

"No, I—"

"And did you hear her friends really have it in for you?" she asked, checking her lip gloss.

"No, I—"

"And do you think these shorts make me look too—".

"Listen, Naomi, I'd really like to chat, but I'm going to be late for class and—"

"I know," she said, "and that's why I'm here."

"Sorry?"

"To help you make it to class without getting killed."

"Killed?" TJ asked.

Naomi lowered her voice and glanced around. "Did you ever see *Jaws*?"

"The movie?"

Naomi nodded. "You need to look at these kids like they're all great white sharks."

"What does that make me?"

"Uhh . . . raw hamburger."

"Hamburger?"

"They say it's a shark's favorite food."

TJ took a breath. "Look, Naomi, I really appreciate you wanting to help and all, but—"

"No sweat," Naomi answered as she adjusted her hair, then readjusted it, then readjusted the readjustment. "That's what best friends do."

"Actually, no offense, but I'm not sure I need a best friend right now." TJ wanted to add "at least not a best friend like you," but since Naomi had enough self-image problems, and TJ didn't want to entirely destroy her life.

"What do you mean?" Naomi asked as they arrived at TJ's locker.

"What I mean is—"

But that's as far as TJ got. Because as she grabbed the locker handle, she finally understood the real reason people had been smiling and snickering at her. It was . . .

PAYBACK TIME.

Now, back in Missouri, a good act of revenge would be to put lard or peanut butter inside someone's locker handle so when they grabbed it, they would get a handful of goo.

Point made, nobody hurt.

But since this was Malibu, California, (where everybody has way too much money) and since it was for Hesper Breakahart (whom everybody was trying way too hard to impress), things were a little different.

Actually, opening the locker was no problem.

It was the 9,207 marbles that came pouring out of it (courtesy of a giant hole someone had drilled through the entire back wall and into her locker, then filled with marbles the night before).

Ever try standing at a locker as 9,207 marbles pour out of it?

Actually, TJ did a pretty good job of standing. It was just all the slipping, sliding, and

"Whoa..."

rolling that made things a little difficult.

Everyone was standing around having a good laugh. Well, everyone but Elizabeth (Hesper's best friend since forever). Instead of laughing, the sweet little thing was offering to help TJ by shouting, "Here, grab this!"

TJ looked up to see Elizabeth holding a fire extinguisher.

"Thanks!" TJ shouted. "But I really don't need that right now!"

"Sure you do," sweet little Elizabeth said.

And before TJ could protest, Elizabeth shoved the giant extinguisher into TJ's arms, pulled the pin, and

wHOOOOOOOOsh

TJ was

"Aughhhhhh..."

shooting down the hall like a NASA rocket to the moon.

Unfortunately, she wasn't heading to the moon. Remember the third-floor fact we were going to get to? Well, as you may have already figured out, third floors always come to an end. And at the end are third-floor . . .

"STAIRS!" TJ shouted. "I'M HEADING FOR THE

bounce . . . bounce . . .
bounce

S-S-STAIRS!"

And as if all that bouncing wasn't bad enough, she heard the familiar and very unwelcome sound of krinkle . . . **krackle**

POOF!

krinkle . . . **krackle**
POOF!

krinkle . . . krackle

POOF!

She glanced over her shoulder and caught a final glimpse of the hallway behind her. It was covered with wall-to-wall flipping and flopping goldfish.

"S-S-STOP TH-TH-THAT!" TJ shouted as she continued down the steps. "T-T-TURN TH-TH-THEM B-B-BACK!"

She didn't have a chance to see if the boys obeyed.

The good news was the bone-jarring flight of steps didn't last forever.

The bad news was there was a *second* flight of bone-jarring steps.

"O-o-o-h-h-h

b-b-b-broth-th-th-er-er-er!"

The good news (if you're keeping track, that's two to one in favor of good news) was that there was somebody at the bottom of the steps who would save her.

"Hang on!" that somebody shouted. "I'll catch you! I'LL CATCH YOU! I'LL—"

thud

"Ooaaaf!"

unconscious crumple to the floor

TJ wasn't sure how long she was knocked out, but when she woke up, she was lying in the arms of her hero.

"Thank you," she said, turning to face him. "Thank you so very—"

This brings us to some more bad news (which ties the score).

"You're (*sniff-sniff*) welcome," her hero said, wiping his nose with the back of his hand and *sniff-sniff*ing again.

That's right, TJ was lying in the arms of Doug Claudlooper, the boy with the perpetual allergies. And since TJ had left all her sweetness and politeness somewhere on the second flight of stairs, she leaped to her feet, staggered backward, and ran away from him screaming.

Unfortunately, things only went downhill from there. (So if you're still keeping score, don't bother. It'll just depress you.)

* * * * *

Chad still couldn't remember the new kid's name. BJ? JT? JB?

Well, whatever it was, she was still her usual non-talkative self.

Since she was his new partner, he was explaining his and Hesper's science fair project. (Actually, it was Hesper's project, since anything involving Hesper was always about Hesper.) And so far the new kid had said a grand total of one word to him—if *uh-huh* can even be considered a word.

"You okay?" he asked.

"Uh-huh," she sorta croaked before ducking behind her long brown hair.

"I heard about your little fall down the steps," he said.

"Uh-huh." The long brown hair nodded.

"You sure you're okay?"

"Uh-huh." More hair nodding.

Although she didn't talk to him, more than once he heard her whispering. Weird things like "No, you cannot help!" and "Don't you dare hurt him!"

Poor thing.

But despite her mental condition, she really was cute. Of course, he could never tell her that. Guys didn't talk that way. They were supposed to talk about gross stuff or football scores. And let's not forget the belching contests. But none of that stuff really interested Chad.

Still, since he was a guy, he was supposed to follow the guy rules.

But there was one guy rule he wouldn't follow. It was common knowledge that if you liked a girl, you were supposed to make fun of her. Chad could never bring himself to do that.

Not with this poor girl. She had enough problems as it was.

"Put that book down!" she hissed.

Poor kid.

Mr. Beaker had stepped out of class to go to the office. Of course he trusted everybody to quietly work on their science projects, so of course everybody was shouting, throwing spit wads, and talking on their cell phones.

Well, almost everybody.

"So," Chad said as they looked into a cage that held their project, a skinny white mouse, "we're investigating how few calories this little guy can eat without dying."

The new kid nodded.

"That's why our pal here—we call him Wendell— is so skinny. I'm no expert, but I think a celery stick a week is pretty cruel."

More nodding.

"Anyway, let's take him from the cage and put him on the scale for weighing."

She nodded and reached into the cage to catch the furry creature.

Chad continued, "Hesper's always worried about what she eats. She's got this thing about staying thin."

More nodding.

"But if you ask me, she's way too skinny. A person who's normal—well, like you—they're a lot better-looking, don't you think?"

Her nodding stopped. Actually, as far as Chad could tell, so did her breathing. Instead, the new kid just sort of stood there, staring at him all wide-eyed and frozen . . . until Wendell slipped from her hands and fell to the floor.

Realizing what happened, she dropped to the floor and began chasing after Wendell. Chad joined her and together, on all fours, they scampered back and forth under the desks and chairs of the science class.

"Over there!" He pointed.

They raced over there.

"Over here!" he shouted.

They raced over here.

It was really kind of funny, the way they kept almost catching Wendell and the way he kept escaping. Pretty soon, Chad was laughing. And pretty soon after that, so was the new kid. It made him feel good, kind of warm inside, to know he was helping her have a little fun. In fact, more than once he let Wendell escape just so they could keep chasing him.

Finally they cornered the little guy.

"Okay," Chad said. "You come at him from the left. I'll come at him from the right."

She nodded.

"On my count. One . . . two . . . three!"

They both lunged forward and they both missed, grabbing each other instead and flopping to the floor, laughing all the harder. Until . . .

Chad noticed they were directly under the desks of two of Hesper's friends—Emma Prinzes and Stephanie Suchasnobb. Besides being majorly stuck on themselves, the two girls were famous for wearing way too much makeup. In fact, the giant black circles around their eyes reminded Chad of raccoons.

But at the moment he wasn't thinking of raccoons. Instead, he was thinking of the half-dozen slimy frogs in the cage the two girls were opening . . . and turning upside down . . . and purposely dumping all over the new kid.

Of course, the new kid went crazy and began screaming, "Get them off! Get them off!"

Of course, the two girls had a good laugh.

And, of course, Chad moved in to help. But as he did, four very strange things happened.

VERY STRANGE THING #1

He heard a weird but somehow familiar sound of . . .

krinkle ... krackle

POOF!

krinkle ...krackle

POOF!

VERY STRANGE THING #2

Stephanie and Emma vanished. Well, not completely. Instead, sitting in their place were two little flies. Except these two little flies wore so much makeup that the weight of all the eyeliner, eye shadow, mascara, lip gloss, and lip liner made it impossible for them to take off.

All they could do was sit there and

buzz ...buzz ...
buzz ...

try.

But stranger than that strangeness was . . .

VERY STRANGE THING #3

A Swiss Army Knife seemed to materialize out of nowhere and clatter to the ground beside the frogs.

And stranger than that strangeness (which was strange enough) was . . .

VERY STRANGE THING #4

Chad heard the frogs talk. It had to be his imagination, but he was sure he heard something like:

"Hey (ribbet-ribbet), check out the delicious meal on those two (ribbet-ribbet) chairs!"

"I don't (ribbet-ribbet) know," another said. **"They look like raccoons."**

"Don't be ridic-(ribbet-ribbet)-ulous. It's dinner!"

The frogs began hopping wildly off the floor, trying to jump to the chairs as the two flies

buzz . . . buzZZZ . . . buzzzZZZ-ed

in panic.

And then, to top off all that stranger-than-strange-ness with just a little more strangeness, the new kid leaped to her feet and shouted, "STOP IT! I TOLD YOU I DON'T WANT YOUR HELP!"

Chad stood up and glanced around. As far as he could tell, there was nobody there. Well, nobody except for the rest of the class, who were all busy staring at her . . . which still didn't stop her shouting:

"TUNA! HERBY! TURN THEM BACK RIGHT NOW!"

Chad shook his head sadly. He had no idea how to help her. Unless, after school, he swung by her house and encouraged her parents to increase her medication.

CHAPTER SEVEN

The Plot Sickens

TIME TRAVEL LOG:
Malibu, California, October 11—supplemental

Begin Transmission:
Subject attempted to cut off communication.
Fortunately her silence is no match for our way-cool
diplomatic skills, and we reestablished dialogue. Plan
to buy cookbook, as her cooking ability is majorly
zworked.

End Transmission

It was TJ's turn to fix dinner. And since they were
out of microwave meals, she had to whip up

something on her own. This would explain all the

crunch, crunch, crunch

gag, gag, gag-ing

you heard around the table.

It's not that TJ was a lousy cook; she just had lots on her mind. So much that she might have over-cooked the meal just a little.

"Well now," Dad said, trying to be positive, "this is quite the dinner. Who would have ever thought of having, um, er, uh . . . What exactly is this we're having, dear?"

"Charcoal dust?" little Dorie asked.

"Fireplace ash?" Violet ventured.

"Mashed potatoes," TJ snapped.

"Ah," Dad said as he subtly slipped a handful under the table for Fido the Wonder Dog. But Fido the Wonder Dog, who will eat anything, was in the living room throwing up. (Apparently Violet had already slipped him a handful of her own "mashed potatoes"—which explained the charcoal dust all over her fingers.)

"So, uh . . ." Dad glanced around, unsure what to do with his handful of dust. "How was everybody's day?"

"I got an A++ on my science test," Violet said, brushing off her hands.

"Hey, that's great!" Dad said. "How do you get *two* pluses?"

"By showing Mrs. Mindbender where she was wrong."

"And she gave you two pluses?" Dorie asked as she hid her charcoal dust under her hamburger patty, which looked more like a burnt hockey puck but didn't taste as good.

"Actually," Violet said, "the other plus came from pointing out where the textbook was wrong."

"I see," Dad said, finally slipping his mashed potato dust into his pants pocket. He turned to TJ and asked, "And tell me, how was your—"

"Fine."

"I see. Did you—"

"Fine!"

"And—"

"FINE!" She jumped to her feet. "Why are you always yelling at me?" She swiped at the tears running down her face. "Everything's fine, all right? FINE, FINE, FINE!"

With that, she spun around and ran up the stairs to her room.

Dad looked on, realizing TJ was anything but fine.

And as soon as he found a place to bury his dinner, nice and deep so Fido wouldn't dig it up (he hated it when family pets died), he'd head upstairs and have a talk with her.

"Violet," he asked, "would you get a plastic garbage bag from the cupboard so we can properly 'finish' our dinner?"

Violet flashed him a grin. "I'm on it." She grabbed her dish and headed for the kitchen.

"I'm right behind you," little Dorie said, scampering after her.

"And make sure it's the triple-ply bags that don't leak," Dad called. "We need to be environmentally friendly."

* * * * *

When TJ threw open the door to her room, there were Tuna and Herby sitting on her desk in their shiny time-travel suits, just as perky as if nothing had ever happened.

"Greetings, earthling." Herby grinned, holding up his hand and spreading his fingers apart.

Tuna explained, "He saw that in one of your old sci-fi movies."

TJ looked at them coolly.

"What?" Herby asked. "You're not a Star Wreck fan?"

Fighting to keep her voice even, she said, "Leave my room and go back to your time pod in the attic. I'm not talking to you."

"Ah, come on, Your Dude-ness." Herby hopped off the desk. "You're not still gur-roid at us about those frogs and flies, are you?"

Her cool look grew cooler.

"We did return them to their original molecular structure," Tuna said.

"Just like we did those goldfish on the third floor," Herby added.

Her cooler look grew colder.

"Come on."

She folded her arms and refused to talk.

The boys exchanged looks. "I believe she really is gur-roid," Tuna said.

Herby nodded. "To the max."

TJ spotted the stack of unopened boxes in the middle of her room. When giving others the silent treatment, it's always best to do something, so she crossed to the boxes and started to unpack.

"So," Tuna said, "I suppose this isn't the best time to point out that you've not improved your behavior with either Naomi Simpletwirp or Doug Claudlooper?"

TJ couldn't believe her ears. Here she was, having the worst week of her life, and all they cared about was how she was treating a couple of loser kids. Amazing. She remained silent and dug into the box.

"Please," Tuna continued, "how is it possible to continue meaningful communication with you if you are unwilling to share your thoughts?"

She gave no answer. Instead she started pulling out clothes her aunt Matilda had packed before they left Missouri—a heavy wool scarf, down-filled parka, thick woolen mittens—just the fashion statements she needed for life in sunny Malibu, California.

Herby nervously cleared his throat. "Do you think she'd, like, mind if we used the Acme Thought Broadcaster?"

"An excellent question." Tuna turned to her. "Do you mind if we utilize our Acme Thought Broadcaster?"

TJ ignored them and continued to dig. Earmuffs, thermal underwear . . .

"That's not exactly a yes," Tuna said.

"But it's not a no, either," Herby said.

Tuna agreed. "Yes, it's not a no, so yes, it could be yes. Yes?"

"Yes." Herby reached into his pocket.

By now TJ was at the bottom of the box. Snow-shoes, battery-powered socks. She was so busy, she didn't see Herby pull out what looked like a ball-point pen. Nor did she hear him give it a click. But she did hear:

zibwaaa . . . zibwaaa . . . zibwaaa

She pulled her head from the box just in time to see an eerie blue beam shooting at her. She tried to duck but was too late. The beam struck her face and immediately she began shouting:

"What is that, what are you doing, what's going on, hey, how come I'm talking but not moving my mouth, wait a minute, my voice is coming from those stereo speakers over there, no way, this is crazy, what's happening, what are you doing, what—?"

"No sweat, Your Dude-ness," Herby said. "It's just our Acme Thought Broadcaster. Sold at 23rd century time-travel stores everywhere."

"Saves the bother of having to speak," Tuna explained.

"A Thought Broadcaster, what, what are you talking about, and how come we're hearing everything I'm thinking, I don't like this, I—"

Tuna frowned. "It appears the thought filter is malfunctioning. She is stuck on maximum broadcast."

"Maximum what, I'm stuck on what, oh yeah, what a surprise, something else of yours that doesn't work, imagine that, is there anything you have that works, and what do you mean by thought filter, what's—"

"Relax," Herby said. "It's nothing to get torked about. It just means we hear *everything* you're thinking."

"Everything I'm thinking, you don't mean everything, boy, it sure sounds like everything, I sure hope you can't hear that I have to go to the bathroom, oh no, I can't believe I just said that, I mean thought it, I mean—"

KNOCK-knock-knock

"TJ?" Dad called from the other side of the door. "Are you okay?"

"Oh no, it's Dad, what do I do, he can't see me like, er, hear me like this, shut it off, shut it—"

"No problemo," Herby whispered. "All I have to do is ... ." He clicked the pen and the blue beam immediately disappeared.

The good news was they no longer heard TJ's thoughts.

The bad news was TJ no longer had any thoughts.

knock-knock-knock

"Sweetheart?"

"Answer him," Tuna whispered.

TJ turned to him and said,

"   ."

She scowled and tried again.

"   !"

"What's her problem?" Herby asked.

"I am uncertain," Tuna answered. "She didn't say."

"Or think," Herby added.

Both boys looked at each other and groaned, "Oh no ..."

"It has also shorted out," Tuna sighed. "We can't hear what she's thinking because she's not thinking."

TJ turned back to him and shouted,
"   !"

knock-knock-knock

"Honey, can we talk?"

The three looked at each other in a panic. (Well, the two boys looked at each other in a panic. TJ was looking at them in a   .)

"Imitate her," Tuna whispered to Herby.

"What?"

"As you did before!"

"Oh, right." Herby cleared his throat and gave another awful impersonation of TJ. "I'm okay, Poppsy."

"Are you sure?"

"Yes. I just need a little time to myself."

"Well, all right," he said. "But I'm here if you need me."

"I know you are."

"And take care of that cold. It sounds like it's getting worse."

"Okay, Poppsy. I love you."

"I love you, too, sweetheart."

Tuna raced to the door and pressed his ear against it until he heard Dad walking away.

Meanwhile, Herby was busy clicking and reclicking the pen, while occasionally

thwack, thwack, thwack-ing

it against the desk, trying to fix it.

All this as TJ stood around, frantically yelling,

"   !"

Suddenly her cell phone rang.

Without thinking (literally), TJ reached into her pocket, pulled out her phone, and answered,

"   ?"

"TJ?" an all-too-familiar voice asked.

"   ," she replied.

"TJ, It's Naomi. Your best new friend."

"   ."

"It must be a bad connection; I can't hear you. But if you can hear me, turn on the TV. Hesper Breakahart is on Eye Witless News, and you won't believe what she's saying."

TJ answered, "   ."

"Sorry. I'll try later. Bye." With that Naomi hung up. TJ turned to Herby, who was still busy

thwack, **thwack, thwack-ing**

the Acme Thought Broadcaster.

She turned to Tuna, who had just pulled something the size of a postage stamp from his pocket. He started unfolding it until it was the size of a notebook. He continued unfolding until it was the size of a computer monitor.

She looked on and would have wondered what he was doing (if her wonderer could wonder) as he continued unfolding it until it was the size of a giant TV (LCD of course). Without a word, he hung it on a nearby wall, clapped his hands twice, and the picture appeared.

There, in all of her plucked-eyebrow, two-hours-of-makeup-and-wardrobe glory, sat Hesper Breakahart. Actually, she wasn't sitting; she was lying in a hospital bed. Both legs were elevated, both arms were in casts, and most of her head was bandaged.

"Yes," she was sobbing, "this is the price one must pay for fame (and having such clear skin)."

The camera zoomed in to a close-up as tears streamed down her face. "But tomorrow I will find the courage to return to school and face my attacker. There I will offer her the olive branch of forgiveness."

"Can you believe this?" Tuna moaned.

Thwack, thwack, *thwack*

Herby *thwack*ed.

Hesper continued, getting her voice to tremble, her bottom lip to quiver, and her eyes to water all at the same time. (She's a professional; what did you expect?) "And perhaps the two of us can live together in world peace and harmony."

Suddenly the beam

zibwaaa . . . zibwaaa . . . zibwaaa

shot from the pen.

"Got it!" Herby shouted in triumph.

"Oh no," TJ moaned in defeat.

Because, even now, as she stared at the TV and her thinker began thinking more thoughtfully . . .

TRANSLATION: *It took a moment before all of her brain cells were finally up to speed.*

Thelma Jean Finkelstein realized the war with Hesper Breakahart wasn't over—not by a long shot.

CHAPTER EIGHT

School Daze

TIME TRAVEL LOG:

Malibu, California, October 12

Begin Transmission:

Subject insisted Tuna and I stay home. How zworked. If she's lucky, she will return from school safe. Then again, we all know about her luck.

End Transmission

There's another little difference between Missouri and Malibu. In Missouri, they don't have television crews running all over the place with cameras.

To be fair, the crew really wasn't running all over

the place; they were just running all over whatever places Hesper Breakahart was being wheeled around.

Wheeled around, as in . . .

"What's she doing in a wheelchair?" TJ asked Naomi as they entered the hallway. Everywhere they looked there were lights and crew members—except directly in front of the camera, where Hesper sat. "I mean, she just has a broken nose."

"Just a broken nose for you," Naomi said as she pulled out a makeup mirror and checked her face. "But for Hesper Breakahart, it's a gold mine."

"What do you mean?"

Naomi put the mirror away. "Follow me."

They pushed their way through the crowd until they got close enough to see dear, darling Hesper, smiling bravely as she wheeled herself toward her locker. It was a touching scene that even had TJ choking up (or gagging), until an older guy with a goatee (which looked more like a hairy patch of bread mold) shouted, "Cut! Cut! Cut!"

Suddenly Hesper's brave, darling smile turned into an angry snarl. "What's wrong with that?" she yelled.

"I need tears, babe," the man said, "lots more tears." He turned around and shouted, "Makeup!"

"Cooming, I em cooming." A woman responded with a French accent (and more hair under her arms than the man had on his face). She dabbed some sort of oil under Hesper's eyes and they immediately started to water.

Meanwhile two other people worked on Hesper's hair.

"It's all for publicity," Naomi explained, pretending to be bored. (She might have pulled it off if she wasn't madly brushing her hair, touching up her lipstick, and applying eyeliner . . . all at the same time.)

Finally the makeup woman shouted, "Vee half tearz! Vee half many, many tearz."

"All right, folks!" the man yelled. "Let's take it from the top. Places, please. And action!"

Once again, darling Hesper rolled toward her locker. But this time she bravely smiled through her many, many tearz.

TJ could only shake her head in disgust, amazement, and—even though she hated to admit it—awe.

* * * * *

An hour later, they were back in Mr. Beaker's science class.

The good news was TJ had convinced Tuna and Herby to stay home and work on their time-travel pod.

The bad news was, well, that Tuna and Herby had stayed home and worked on their time-travel pod.

She had no sooner sat down beside Chad (which was a good thing 'cause her knees were still a little weak around him) when the door opened and in rolled Hesper.

"Oh, Hesper!" Elizabeth, her best friend since forever, cried. "You've joined us!"

Hesper looked up and smiled bravely (she was getting a lot of mileage out of smiling bravely) when another student rose to her feet and started to clap. Another student also stood and clapped. And then another and another, until the entire class was on their feet giving Hesper Breakahart a standing ovation.

It seemed a little over-the-top, even for Hesper, until TJ noticed the film crew coming in the door behind her.

"Thank you." Hesper bowed her head humbly. "Thank you." Then she looked up and gave (what else?) a brave smile. "Thank you; oh, thank you, thank you, thank you."

When everyone was finished and finally took their seats, things returned to normal—well, as normal as anything can be with a TV star, a TV crew . . . and an old, wannabe actor.

That's right. You see, Mr. Beaker was still standing. In his hands he held a clipboard. And on the clipboard was what looked like a script that he pretended not to read:

"Dear *sweet* and lovely *Hesper*." (He obviously needed a few more acting lessons.) Mr. Beaker looked up and searched the class until he found Hesper sitting right in front of him. He cranked up his mouth into what was supposed to be a smile. The camera moved in closer as he looked back at the clipboard, pretending not to read what he was obviously reading.

"You *are* so brave returning to *my* class so soon *after* all you have been *through*." He looked up and gave her another smile.

Hesper returned the smile, which seemed to be wilting as his awful performance continued.

"You *are* so brave returning to *my* class so soon *after* all you—" He frowned and pretended not to search the clipboard until he pretended not to find his place.

"Dear *sweet* and lovely *Hesper*—" More frowning and more pretending not to search. "Oh," he said, pretending not to put his finger on the script so he'd not lose his place. "Your absence has *been* so greatly appreciated *and* felt— No, I mean, your absence has **been** so greatly **felt** and we **appreciate** your returning so soon."

"*Psst.*" The man with the hairy chin waved. "Faster, faster!"

Mr. Beaker nodded and glanced back down at the clipboard. "As a **token** of our appreciation, I have re-**assigned** you to your old lab partner to continue what I'm sure will **be** an award-winning science fair pro-**ject**."

Once again the class broke into applause.

Mr. Beaker looked up and smiled. "Thank you." He seemed uncertain what to do, so he snuck in a quick little bow. "Thank you."

Hesper wiped her eyes in gratitude (either for the reassignment or because the man's performance was finally over). Bravely, she rolled toward Chad.

TJ couldn't believe her eyes (or the number of times she'd heard the word *brave*).

Chad raised his hand. "Mr. Beaker?" he asked.

The teacher glanced to him, then down to the script, looking for his place.

Chad continued, "What about BJ, er, JT?"

Mr. Beaker looked up. "Who?"

"The new kid."

The class grew so quiet you could hear a press-on fingernail drop.

"What about her?" Mr. Beaker asked.

"Who will be . . . ?" Chad swallowed. He seemed uncharacteristically nervous about the TV camera (and Hesper's eyes boring into him). "Who will be her lab partner?"

TJ's face reddened. The class murmured. And Mr. Beaker madly searched his script for an answer.

Fortunately, another student was there to help.

Unfortunately, the other student was looking longingly at TJ while *sniff*ing, *snuff*ing, and wiping his nose on the back of his hand.

"I don't have a partner," Doug Claudlooper said. "She can be mine."

*   *   *   *   *

The rest of the class period was about the same, except for the part about it being a whole lot worse.

First there was the problem of Doug Claudlooper. TJ had spent all period listening to him explain the robot kitten he was completing (actually, *they* were completing) for the science fair.

"This gear is connected to this (*sniff*) gyro, which is connected to this (*snuff*) girder, which is connected to this . . ."

Eventually, his voice became nothing but a blur of words:

"Connected current battery (*sniff*) electrical of the parallel to the cells servo (*snuff*) motor wiring interconnected circuits . . ."

Then it became a blur of sounds:

"Stateoftheartengineering(*sniff*)connectedthrough opticalportaloptions(*snuff*)inwhichcasetheymustbein perfectphaseandalignmenttothe . . ."

But through sheer politeness, TJ managed not to fall asleep and to actually "Mm-hm," "I see," and "Uh-huh" her way through his explanations until the bell finally rang.

Unfortunately, Doug wasn't exactly finished. Which meant following her into the hall, sniffing, snuffing, and

"It'scooltofinallyfindsomeonewhoknowsandunder standswhatI'mdoingespeciallygirlscausesomeofthem aren'tsosmartas—"

"Uh, listen, Doug," she interrupted. "I need to go to the restroom."

"I can wait," he sniffed.

"No, that's all right."

"Oh, well, maybe I'll see you later," he snuffed.

"Yeah, right," she muttered, turning for the restroom, "after I graduate, go to college, get married, have kids, and have a hundred grandkids . . ."

"Funny," Doug called after her.

She turned to him.

He was trying to smile, but it was obvious he'd overheard her. "About the grandkids," he said.

TJ felt her face grow hot. "Oh, Doug, I didn't mean—"

"No, don't worry about it," he said, still trying to smile. "I get that all the time."

"Doug, I didn't mean—"

"No (*sniff*) problem," he said. "Guess I'll see you in class tomorrow."

"Doug . . ."

He turned, gave a little wave, and (*snuff*) disappeared into the crowd.

Great, she thought, *just great. What else could go wrong?*

But as you've probably already guessed, she was about to find out.

* * * * *

Everybody in Malibu Junior High bought lunch (or had it catered in by their private chefs). Everybody, that is, except TJ.

"A penny saved is a penny earned," Dad said. "It all adds up."

> **TRANSLATION:** *TJ and her sisters always brown-bagged their lunches to school.*

TRANSLATION OF TRANSLATION: *TJ had packed some of last night's leftovers. (Apparently Dad hadn't buried it all.)*

TRANSLATION OF TRANSLATION OF TRANSLATION: *TJ planned to be choking down charcoal potatoes and an overcooked hockey puck.*

But that was the least of her worries.

"Hey!" Naomi shouted as TJ entered the crowded cafeteria. "Over here!"

TJ turned to see the tall, gangly girl sitting by herself.

"I managed to save room at my table!" she called.

Actually, Naomi always managed to save room at her table (since no one ever sat at her table).

TJ glanced nervously around, looking for some other place, for *any* other place.

"Over here!" Naomi waved both of her arms. "Plenty of room here!" (The poor thing had obviously not mastered the fine art of being subtle . . . or cool.)

TJ searched the room one last time.

"OVER HERE!" Naomi stood on her chair, waving her arms and shouting. (She'd definitely not mastered the fine art of being subtle.) "I SAVED YOU A SEAT OVER HERE!"

TJ turned to her, managed a smile (which felt more like a grimace), and started forward.

But she'd taken only a few steps before she heard, "Oh, there she is now!" It was a syrupy sweet voice (that, of course, sounded brave). "Over here, um, er, whatever your name is!"

TJ looked across the room to see a perfectly manicured hand waving at her. It was attached to a perfectly bronzed arm that was attached to the perfect body of . . . Hesper Breakahart.

"Over here," she called from her wheelchair. "We've got plenty of room!"

TJ slowed to a stop. Even from across the cafeteria, Hesper's blinding white grin was . . . well, blindingly white.

"TJ!" Naomi shouted.

TJ looked back to Naomi, then over to Hesper. Suddenly she was torn with indecision.

"What are you doing?" Naomi called. "She hates you, remember?"

TJ did remember. But sitting directly beside Hesper Breakahart was Chad Steel . . . and all the other cooler-than-cool kids.

"Over here!" Hesper continued to call and flash her blinding white smile.

And let's not forget the camera crew. Not that TJ wanted to be a star or anything, but imagine what it would be like to be on national TV. Imagine what her friends back in Missouri would think when they saw her hanging out with Hesper Breakahart.

"TJ?" Naomi called. "TJ?!"

Finally, she made her decision. Without a word, TJ turned and headed for Hesper's table.

Once again she felt all eyes turning toward her, and once again she felt her face growing hot. Only this time it was a good type of hot.

Closer and closer she came.

Bigger and bigger Hesper smiled. "I'm sooo glad you could join us," she said.

TJ nodded.

"And that there are no hard feelings."

TJ nodded some more. Out of the corner of her eye, she saw the camera crew moving in for a close-up.

"And I just want you to know that no matter how jealous you may be over my fame and incredible good looks, I completely forgive you."

The words struck TJ as odd. Odder still was what the man with the hair on his chin was shouting: "A little louder, babe, a little louder."

Hesper nodded and repeated more loudly, "And

no matter how jealous you may be over my fame and incredible good looks, I completely forgive you!" She cranked up her grin to ultra-blind. "And I want us to be best friends forever." With that, she stuck out her hand.

TJ wasn't sure if she was supposed to shake it, curtsy, or kiss her ring. Since Hesper wasn't old enough to be the queen (or the pope), she decided on the handshake. So as she arrived at the table, she stuck out her right hand—an unfortunate decision, since that was the hand that also held her lunch sack.

Even more unfortunate, because that lunch sack held the burnt hamburger patty and charcoal potatoes.

And *most* unfortunate, because as she stuck out her hand to shake, the contents flew out of the bag.

Suddenly everything seemed to turn into slow motion, like a bad movie:

"OOohhh, nOOOO . . . ,"

TJ cried in horror as the food floated out of her sack.

"Gaaaasssspppp . . . ,"

the crowd gasped as the hamburger patty raced toward Hesper's face.

Ker-Spppplaaaaaaattt . . .

the hamburger patty *ker-splatt*ed as it hit Hesper in the mouth, knocking out both of her front teeth.

"Aaaa hooockeeeey puuuuuck?! Shhhheeeee hiiiiit meeeee wiiiithhhh a hoooooockeeeey puuuuuuuck??!!"

Hesper cried.

Then everything turned back to normal speed, including . . .

—All the kids screaming.
—Hesper dropping to her knees and searching the floor, crying, **"Ma teeph! Waare's ma teeph!"**
—And four (count them, *four!*) burly teachers grabbing TJ and dragging her away.

TJ wanted to explain, but it's hard explaining when people are shouting such understanding words as

Teacher One: "How dare you attack a defenseless girl!"
Teacher Two: "Who just happens to be a superstar!"
Teacher Three: "You're lucky we don't call the police!"
Teacher Four: "Or Oprah!"

All of this as Elizabeth, Hesper's best friend since forever, had flipped open her cell phone and was screaming, "What's the number for 911? What's the number for 911?!"

Amid the chaos, TJ looked over to Chad, who stared sadly after her, shaking his head. Along with *crazy* he had no doubt added *dangerous* to her list of personality traits.

Extremely dangerous.

CHAPTER NINE

T Minus One Day and Counting . . .

TIME TRAVEL LOG:
Malibu, California, October 13

Begin Transmission:
Subject seems to be on verge of learning lesson . . . if she survives!

End Transmission

Chad stared out his window at the neighbor's front lawn. It was supposed to be night. But with all the TV crews, lights, and a circling helicopter (or two), you'd never know it.

Talk about a circus. No wonder the new kid and

her family were locked up in their house with the shades drawn.

Earlier, the six o'clock news had run a special report: *Star Stalker Stalks Star*

where they showed what happened in the cafeteria about a hundred times—first in slow motion, then in stop action, then in reverse action, then in every type of action you could imagine (though the reenactment with hand puppets was a little much).

Poor kid. He really felt sorry for her.

It got even worse when she and her dad went outside and talked to the reporters. They must have figured explaining the truth would help. But who was interested in truth when a star stalker was stalking stars? (Say that ten times fast.)

"So tell us, BJ," the first reporter had asked.

"That's TJ," her dad corrected.

"Right, so tell us, JT, when did you first decide to attack Hesper Breakahart?"

The new kid answered, "I didn't decide to attack her."

"Oh, it just happened, like you couldn't control yourself."

"No, it didn't just happen."

"So how long were you planning it?"

"Planning?" she asked.

"To beat her up like that."

"I didn't beat her up like that."

"Then how *did* you beat her up?"

When it was clear nobody cared about the truth, her dad finally took her inside and closed the door. But the reporters didn't go away. Soon they were swarming all over her yard.

One even began digging in her lawn.

"Hey, look what I found!" he shouted from beside the fence.

Chad craned his neck to see the reporter holding a shovel in one hand and an extra-thick, triple-ply garbage bag in the other.

"What's in it?" someone yelled.

The man opened it, gave a sniff, and nearly passed out. Coughing and gasping for breath, he shouted, "Whatever it is, it must be toxic! Hey, wait a minute." He rummaged in the bag. "This is where she stores her weapons."

"You're kidding!" another reporter shouted.

"No. I'm counting two—make that three—of those burnt hockey pucks!"

"Fantastic!"

"Better call the bomb squad."

But the reporters weren't just swarming over the new kid's yard and digging through her trash. One reporter and his cameraman had actually crawled onto her roof and were sneaking around.

That was it. Chad had seen enough. He rapped loudly on his window and shouted, "Hey . . . hey!"

The reporter and his cameraman looked up, startled.

Chad unlatched his window and opened it. "What do you think you're doing?"

"Shh," the reporter whispered. He motioned toward the new kid's bedroom window. "We're going to get a shot of her planning her next attack."

"You can't do that!"

"Right," the reporter said. "Watch me."

"Get down from there!" Chad demanded.

But they ignored him. No way would they listen to some kid.

Chad turned and started toward his door. They may not listen, but if he went out there and physically dragged them off the roof, they'd pay attention. Unfortunately, he'd barely stepped into his hallway before he heard a weird and oddly familiar *krinkle* . . . . *krackle*

POOF!

krinkle . . . . **krackle**

POOF!

He raced back to his bedroom window. The reporter and the cameraman had completely disappeared. The camera was still there. So was the microphone. But instead of two men . . .

Chad closed his eyes and shook his head. When he reopened them, nothing had changed. Instead of two men, there were now two kangaroos hopping around on the roof. Two kangaroos who looked very frightened and very, very confused.

* * * * *

The following day Tuna and Herby had to convince TJ to go back to school.

"Everybody hates me," she argued as she shuffled down the stairs to breakfast. (It was Violet's turn to cook, which meant everything would be healthy . . . and impossible to eat.)

"Not Doug and Naomi," Tuna said. "They don't hate you."

TJ gave him a look. "And that's supposed to make me feel better?"

"It will," Herby giggled.

"What's that supposed to mean?"

The boys exchanged knowing glances.

"Oh yeah," she said. "You're from the future, so you can tell me what's going to happen, right?"

"Right, but wrong," Herby said.

"Can, but won't," Tuna agreed. "However, we may continue to remind you about the lesson you are currently learning."

"Lesson?" TJ asked.

"Regarding how one should not show favoritism."

"Favoritism?"

"Yeah, how you totally treat Chad and Hesper like royalty—"

"—and Doug and Naomi like beggars."

TJ sighed wearily as they reached the bottom of the stairs. She'd almost forgotten their earlier lecture.

As they headed toward the kitchen, Herby continued. "No offense, Your Dude-ness, but you have to be, like, the world's slowest learner."

"Come on, guys," she argued, "Doug and Naomi—they're so, so . . ."

"Doug-ish and Naomi-ish?" Herby asked.

"Well, yeah."

Tuna cleared his throat and quoted: "'Love your neighbor as yourself.' But if you favor some people over others, you are committing a sin."

She turned to him and frowned. "That sounds like something I've heard in church."

"It should; it's in the Bible."

"Whoa, you guys still use the Bible?" she asked.

"Of course," Herby said. "We're not totally torked."

"That's a matter of opinion," TJ muttered.

"Pardon me?" Dad asked, looking up from his morning paper.

"Nothing," TJ said as she arrived and pulled out a chair. Before her sat a dozen dishes of fried grass, poached celery, scrambled birch bark, and three different types of organically grown mold.

Violet had really outdone herself this time.

"Listen, sweetheart," Dad said, "with all the drama going on right now, if you want to skip school today, I'll certainly understand." He reached over and poured himself another cup of steaming pinesap.

TJ looked hopefully across the table, where Herby

and Tuna sat invisible—well, invisible to everyone but her. Both were shaking their heads.

"So what do you think?" Dad asked.

The boys shook their heads more violently.

Reluctantly, TJ answered, "That's okay, Daddy, I think I'll go."

"Are you sure?"

She glanced back to the guys, who were nodding and grinning.

"Yeah," she said, "I'm sure. Besides, maybe I'll actually learn something." Then, under her breath, she muttered, "I'd better."

* * * * *

"And since we have finally come upon the final day to finally finish your science fair projects . . ." Mr. Beaker stood before the class doing what he did best—boring everyone to tears (or at least to sleep).

TJ tried her best to listen, but it's hard listening when you're busy

zzZZZZ . . .

dozing off every few seconds.

". . . gather your projects and proceed directly to the gymnasium, where the judges will begin judging first thing tomorrow morning and where, if you are fortunate enough to . . ."

It's not just that Mr. Beaker was boring, but you could make millions selling his voice. Forget tranquilizers or sleeping pills—just drop in a CD of Mr. Beaker and everyone would immediately nod off.

". . . and furthermore and therefore and so forth and so on . . ."

TJ wasn't sure how long she'd been asleep before she was startled awake by something rubbing against her leg and the quiet

PUrrrrr-ing

of a cat.

She looked down to see Doug's mechanical kitten at her feet. Talk about cute. It still looked like a robot, with all the steel and stuff, but he'd added a pair of little ears and furry pipe-cleaner whiskers. It really was cute. And in its little mouth it held a card.

TJ glanced up to Mr. Beaker, who was still

furthermoring, thereforing, and so-forthing. She
reached down to take the card and read:

I didn't mean to be a bother.
Can we start over just as friends?

She looked across the room and saw Doug oper-
ating the remote controls. It was a sweet gesture and
she had to smile. He smiled back. Not all goofy and
weird like before. More like . . . well, like a friend.

And when Mr. Beaker had finally finished (by put-
ting himself to sleep), she got up and joined Doug.

"So what do you think?" he sniffed.

She looked down to the kitten. "I think he's really
cute."

"He's a she," Doug corrected.

"Oh, and does she have a name?"

"I call her TJ." He beamed.

TJ frowned and fidgeted.

He winced. "A little much?"

She nodded. "A little much."

"Sorry. Then how 'bout Killer?"

"Killer?" She giggled. "For a kitten?"

"Sure."

"She doesn't look like a killer."

"Ah—" Doug grinned—"but looks can be deceiving." He pressed another button on his remote control and out of the cute little mouth came a gigantic little

ROAR!!!

It was so loud, it woke up everyone in the class (including Mr. Beaker). And it was so funny, TJ broke out laughing. Everybody in the room turned to glare at her (Big Surprise #1). And they all tried to make her feel small and stupid (Big Surprise #2). But it was so funny, she didn't care. For the first time since she'd started school, she didn't care what anybody thought. And it felt terrific.

"So," Doug sniffed, "shall we take her to the gym and set up the display?"

TJ motioned to the hall. "Let's do it."

He nodded, pushed a few more levers, and the three of them headed toward the door. Of course, everyone was still staring, so of course, Doug pressed the button and Killer gave another, even louder

as they headed out of the room and down the hall, laughing all the way.

* * * * *

Chad watched them leave the room. He couldn't help smiling, pleased that the new kid had finally found a friend. His cell phone vibrated and he opened it to read the text. It was from Hesper.

GOOD NEWZ. HIRED A TEAM OF SCIENTISTS 2 FIX OUR SCI FAIR PROJECT

Chad texted back:

FIX?

She answered:

THEYRE ADDING A LASER BEAM WILL B READY TOMORROW

Chad blinked at the screen.

LASER BEAM? ON A MOUSE??

Hesper answered with a final message:

NOBODY MESSES WITH ME.
UR GONNA LOVE IT!!!
XOXOXXO

Chad stared at the message. The good feeling he had for the new kid suddenly didn't feel so good. With Hesper on the warpath, it didn't feel good at all.

CHAPTER TEN

Show and ~~Tell~~ YELL!

TIME TRAVEL LOG:

Malibu, California, October 14

Begin Transmission:

If you thought things were bad before . . .

End Transmission

For the first time that week, TJ almost felt good about going to school.

Almost.

She would have felt better if the two boys hadn't insisted on tagging along.

"Trust us, Your Dude-ness," Herby said, floating invisibly beside her. "You'll want us with you."

"Why today?" she asked as they headed up the sidewalk toward the gymnasium. "I don't get it."

"Oh, you will." Tuna gave a heavy sigh. "I'm afraid you'll understand in a very big way."

She opened the gym doors and came to a stop. Before her were rows and rows of science projects. Of course there were the usual ones thrown together by last-minute slackers. Like the experiment with a giant hammer and a huge crate of tomatoes titled

HOW MANY TIMES CAN YOU HIT A TOMATO WITH A SLEDGEHAMMER BEFORE IT SPLATTERS?

RESULTS: Once (unless you're a very bad shot).

Or the one with all the gauze and first aid cream titled

WHAT HAPPENS IF YOU HOLD YOUR HAND OVER A CANDLE FLAME FOR FIVE MINUTES?

RESULTS: You scream until you pass out.

But there were plenty of other experiments asking questions only the super-spoiled and super-rich could have. Like the project with the recording of a barking dog. Its title was

WHICH DESIGNER JEWELRY MAKES POODLES THE HAPPIEST?
RESULTS: Whatever has the most diamonds.

Or the project with a giant pile of ash in a wheelbarrow titled

DO $50 BILLS BURN FASTER THAN $100 BILLS?
RESULTS: After several hundred tries, results are undetermined.

"TJ!" a voice called. "Over here!"

She turned to see Doug standing in the section especially set aside for inventions. At his feet was Killer, the mechanical kitten.

TJ waved and headed to join them. As she approached, she saw other inventions that only the super-spoiled and super-rich could dream up:

THE AUTOMATIC HAND RAISER
Stop the bother of raising your hand in class!

Simply press a button and it automatically pops up for you.

(Batteries not included)

or

AUTOMATIC CATALOG ORDERER
Never bother having to decide what to buy from expensive catalogs again.

Just press SELECT ALL and this device will order everything!

TJ arrived and bent down to scoop up the purring kitten. The little thing was cuter than ever. She glanced around the gym. "Looks like we've got some pretty stiff competition," she said.

Suddenly a bright light blazed from the far corner of the gym.

"What's that?" she asked.

Doug pushed up his glasses and sniffed. "I'll give you one guess. Come on."

They crossed the gym to investigate. Along the way, they passed other rich-kid inventions like

GIANT MIRROR SURFBOARD
Check out your do while checking out the waves!

and more experiments like

WHICH CAVIAR DO HAMSTERS LIKE BEST?
RESULTS: The most expensive you can find.

At last they arrived to see Hesper Breakahart holding another press conference under the bright lights. Chad stood silently beside her, just as uncomfortable as ever. And between them, on a control panel, was their skinny little mouse, Wendell. The poor critter had something strapped to his head that looked like a miniature flashlight.

They listened as Hesper spoke to the crowd.

"What we did was attach a laser to the side of cute little Wendell's head. So wherever he looks, he can fire a laser beam."

"That's *in*-credible, Hes-*per*," a bald reporter said. (His acting was as bad as Mr. Beaker's.)

"Yes." She nodded. "I think so."

"Where did *you* come up with *such* an incredible ide-*a*?"

"Oh, I just wanted to help our brave soldiers overseas." She flashed a brand-new smile with brand-new false teeth. "Of course, the hardest part was all the work Chad and I had to do to build this laser. Isn't that right, Chad?"

Chad's gaze landed on TJ, and he hesitated.

"Isn't that right, Chad?" Before he could answer, Hesper held out her hand with a pout. "I mean, I almost broke a nail. See."

The crowd sighed in sympathy.

Chad looked down in embarrassment.

The reporter asked, "So **may** we have a demonstra-**tion**?"

"Why, certainly." She looked over to Chad. "Chad, sweetie?"

Without a word, he obediently picked up Wendell.

Hesper reached for the control panel. "All I have to do is press a little button labeled POWER ON." She searched the box trying to find where her scientists put it. "Ah, here we go. I just press this little button like so, and—"

Instantly the control panel hummed to life. So did the laser strapped to Wendell's head. It frightened the little guy so badly that he leaped out of Chad's hands and raced across the floor.

That was the good news.

That bad news was that everywhere it jerked its little head, the laser

ZAAAAAAP-ed

And I do mean *everywhere*.
The skylights . . .

ZAAAAAAP
    Crash! Tinkle, tinkle, tinkle
(Which, of course, is the sound of falling glass.)

the people . . .

zAAAAAAP

    "Yikes!"
    (Which, of course, is the sound a judge makes
when his pants are set on fire.)

and

zAAAAAAP

    "Eeeeek!"
    (Which, of course, is the sound a teacher makes
when her wig is set on fire.)

    But it wasn't just skylights and people. Even the
science fair exhibits were hit.

HOW MANY TIMES CAN YOU HIT A TOMATO WITH A SLEDGEHAMMER?

became

zAAAAAaP

WHAT ARE WE GOING TO DO WITH ALL THIS KETCHUP?!

Then, the second-worst of all worsts happened. (The worst of all worsts is coming up in the next chapter.) Little Wendell the mouse spotted little Killer the kitty. And since Wendell was now a major weapon of mass destruction, the little furball went after Killer with everything he had.

ZAAAAAAP! ZAAAAAAP! ZAAAAAAP!

Normally, this wouldn't have been a problem. I mean it's only a mechanical kitty, right (despite the cute pipe-cleaner whiskers)? The problem was that TJ still held Killer in her arms. And since TJ had a thing for living, she took off screaming. She ran this way and that.

ZAAAAAAP!

ZAAAAAAP!

ZAAAAAAP!

Then that way and this.

ZAAAAAAP! ZAAAAAAP!
ZAAAAAAP!

She could have just set Killer down, but it's hard remembering those types of details when you're screaming and running for your life.

Seeing the problem, Chad took off to catch the mouse.

Meanwhile, Hesper was yelling such helpful things as, "Don't break the laser; we want to get an A!"

"Tuna!" TJ cried. "Herby, where are you?"

"That's our cue!" Tuna shouted from the corner where they'd been watching.

"I'm on it!" Herby yelled. He reached for his Swiss Army Knife, pulled open the blade, and fired the Morphing Beam directly at the little mouse.

krinkle . . . krackle
POOF!

Sadly, at that exact moment, Wendell turned left as Herby fired right. Sadder still, Chad didn't.

TRANSLATION: *Chad Steel just became a giant chunk of cheddar cheese.*

Worse yet, he smelled like a giant chunk of cheddar cheese. Which explains why Wendell skidded to a halt, sniffed the air, and spun around. It also explains why he charged after Chad with all the hunger of a starving mouse who had only been fed a celery stick once a week.

"Stop him!" TJ shouted. "Somebody stop him!"

Herby changed knife blades and fired again. The good news was he

krinkle . . . krackle
POOF!

finally hit Wendell. The bad news was, instead of one Wendell, there were now

krinkle . . . krackle

POOF!

two.

krinkle . . . krackle

POOF!

Make that four.
"What's going on?!" Tuna shouted.
"The Duplication Blade!" Herby yelled. "It's stuck!"

krinkle . . . krackle

POOF!

krinkle . . . krackle

POOF!

krinkle . . . krackle
POOF!

Soon, dozens of the little mice were running around, and every one of them was

ZAAAAAAP! ZAAAAAAP! ZAAAAAAP!-ing

as they raced toward Chad for a major cheese feast.

TJ spun toward Hesper and shouted, "Turn off the power!"

And sweet, lovely Hesper screeched back, "I don't know how! I didn't make this stupid thing!"

Meanwhile, everybody in the gym was screaming, running for their lives, and busy having a heart attack or two.

Everyone but Doug.

CHAPTER ELEVEN

Worst of all Worsts

TIME TRAVEL LOG:

Malibu, California, October 14—supplemental

Begin Transmission:
Oops . . .

End Transmission

"Augh!"

Doug ripped down the giant mirror surfboard and raced toward the circle of Wendells that were closing in on Chad. TJ couldn't believe her eyes. It was like he was a superhero the way he leaped into the center of things.

Of course they began firing at him, but each time they

ZAAAAAAP! ZAAAAAAP! ZAAAAAAP!-ed

their lasers, he blocked the beams with the surfboard. Not only blocked them but used the mirror to reflect the beams right back at them, which explains the

K-blewie! k-blewie! k-blewie!

of him blowing up the little critters and sending them to that big cheese fondue party in the sky.

(Actually, he didn't kill them; he just made them unconscious in an *I don't think they'll be waking up anytime soon* kind of way.)

In fact, he was doing such a good job that it looked like the catastrophe would soon be over . . . except for the part of Tuna and Herby wanting to help.

"Quick!" Tuna shouted. "Employ the Enlarge-o Beam!"

"What?" Herby yelled.

"On the kitten. Increase its size so it will attack the mice."

"Good thinking," Herby said. He pulled out what looked like a paper clip and pointed it at Killer, who was still in TJ's arms.

This time she was smart enough to drop the mechanical kitten.

Unfortunately, Herby wasn't smart enough to use the right setting. Instead of the usual 4.5 setting for **NORMAL BIG,** he cranked it all the way up to 9.5 for **ULTRA BIG!** A beam shot from the paper clip with yet another strange

kazoobwa... *kazoobwa*...

sound until, suddenly, Killer was twice her size.

kazoobwa...
kazoobwa...

Better make that four times her size.

kazoobwa . . .
kazoobwa . . .

All right, she just kept getting bigger, okay? In fact, before you could say, "Will these guys ever learn?" Killer was the size of a semitruck (without the cool mud flaps and air horn).

And she wanted to play.

Unfortunately there were no balls of yarn or chew toys. But there were plenty of chew bleachers . . . chew science projects . . . and a chew news reporter.

Carefully, the reporter backed away from her. "Nice kitty-kitty," he said.

"ROAR!"

nice kitty-kitty roared. Then she took a playful swat at him. Well, playful for her. For him, it was more like a giant battering ram that

WHAM!

knocked him completely across the gym.

TJ spun around to Tuna and shouted, "Do something!"

But Tuna was too busy shouting at Herby, who was too busy fumbling with the paper clip.

"The Acme Thought Broadcaster!" Herby yelled. "We'll talk with her mind through the Acme Thought Broadcaster!"

"She's a robot!" Tuna shouted. "She doesn't have a mind!"

But Herby wasn't about to be confused with facts. He reached for the ballpoint pen and fired the eerie blue beam. Unfortunately, he missed the cat and hit Doug's mirror surfboard. Not a problem, except it reflected off the surfboard and landed squarely on Hesper Breakahart. Suddenly they heard, *"Oh, my hair, I think it's out of place, is my nose too shiny, I think my lips are drying, where's that stupid makeup lady with the hairy armpits . . . ?"*

Now, for those of you keeping track, we have:

—one hysterical TV star
—one chunk of Chad Cheddar Cheese

—one hero using a mirror surfboard to fight off
—a bunch of mice with laser beams strapped to
    their heads
—and one very cute mechanical kitty on a not-
    very-cute mechanical rampage

And now you can add that the room was filled
with a loud

BARK BARK BARK-ing

"Oh no," TJ groaned, "what do we have now,
a giant dog?"
    But it wasn't a dog. It was Naomi Simpletwirp!
She stood next to the

WHICH DESIGNER JEWELRY MAKES POODLES THE HAPPIEST?

exhibit. She held the news reporter's microphone
and had shoved it right next to the speaker with the
recording of the barking poodle. Moments before,
she had used all her geeky AV skills to wire the
sound into the school's intercom system. And now,
every room and every hallway in the school was
filled with its barking.

The mechanical kitten froze in fear. She looked this way and that. But the barking came from every direction. Filled with terror, she turned and bolted for the nearest door, which was about three sizes too

CRASH!

small.

Poor Killer the kitty went to pieces . . . literally. Broken gears and steel girders flew in all directions. Wherever you looked, pieces of the robot were raining down. Soon the gym was covered in junk. (Almost as bad as little Dorie's room. Well, not quite, but you get the picture.)

All of this as Doug

K-blewie!-ed

the last of the Wendells with the reflected beam . . . and Herby was finally able to morph Chad back into

krinkle . . . krackle
POOF!

a 1976 Ford pickup. Er,

krinkle . . . **krackle POOF!**

a giant wad of used chewing gum. No,

krinkle . . . **krackle POOF!**

a very confused (but still great-looking) neighbor, who had the faint aroma of dairy products.

Unbelievable. But at last, it had come to an end. Everything began to settle down and return to normal. Well, everything except Hesper Breakahart . . .

"I hate this science fair, I hate this school, everyone's such a loser, wait a minute, is that me, how can people hear what I'm thinking, no way, they're too stupid to know what I really think about their pathetic little lives—"

That's right. The Acme Thought Broadcaster Beam was stuck, and all of Hesper's thoughts were being broadcast through the school.

"And now I'm going to have to talk all nicey nicey to

*that ignorant Mr. Beaker to make sure he gives me an A,
talk about a lamebrain, can you believe he actually likes
Coach Steroidson, I mean if she was any uglier they'd
have to buy her a dog license—"*

"Tuna!" TJ hissed. "Herby! Fix it!"

"We're trying!" Herby said as he began

thwack thwack thwack-ing

the pen on the floor.

Meanwhile, Doug and Chad stared at each other,
completely confused.

"What just happened?" Chad asked.

"I'm . . . not certain," Doug said, pushing up his
glasses.

They both turned to TJ, who tried to smile.
Then they looked over to Naomi, who stood by the
speaker still holding the microphone.

"I'm sorry about your science project," Naomi
called over to Doug. "But I had to do something to
stop it."

"No," Doug sniffed, "you were . . . That was great."

She gave an embarrassed shrug. "Just your average
AV stuff."

"No, that was . . ." Doug approached her. He was

definitely impressed. "That was incredible. I had no idea you could do those types of things."

Naomi's face reddened and she looked down, giving another shrug.

"You want to show me how you did it?" he asked. "I mean, that was really (*sniff*) cool. Really, really cool."

She looked up at him and smiled. "Yeah?"

He smiled back. "Yeah."

TJ watched them and also had to smile. Talk about the perfect couple.

"Hey, you okay?"

She turned to see Chad walking up to her.

"Yeah," she sort of croaked. "How 'bout you?"

He shook his head. "I don't know. It was like I fell asleep and had another one of those strange dreams."

Meanwhile, Hesper's thoughts continued to echo through the school: "*Chad, you stupid boy toy, why are you talking to that ugly new girl, you know I own you, I can have any boy I want in this lame-o school 'cause they're all so stupid, so get over here and start waiting on me hand and foot—*"

TJ threw a look to Chad, who appeared anything but happy.

But Hesper was already cranking up her smile to

the news reporter who'd been cowering in the corner. *"And you ignorant newspeople, if you had any idea
what I really think of you and how I manipulate you to
get whatever I want just because I'm incredibly beautiful
and popular and—"*

Chad shook his head. "Weird. Very, very weird."

TJ nodded. "Yeah."

They spotted Doug and Naomi starting to pick up
broken pieces of the mechanical kitten.

"You guys need a hand?" Chad called.

But the couple was so busy talking and gawking
at each other, they didn't hear.

Chad gave a chuckle. So did TJ. And then,
together, without a word, they started to help.

All of this as TJ's invisible pals continued another
in-depth discussion:

"You've really zworked this up, dude. Now we're
in total quod-quod."

"It is certainly not my fault our tools keep shorting
out."

"It is too."

"It is not."

"Is too."

"Is not."

"I know you are but what am I."

"That makes absolutely no sense."

"Does too."

"Does not."

TJ let out a quiet sigh. It was true. Things *were* weird. But even as weird as this weirdness was, she suspected the weirdness of her future weirdness would be even weirder.

TRANSLATION: *It was only the beginning.*

CHAPTER TWELVE

Wrapping Up

Lunch that day was a little different.

Of course TJ had the same old sack lunch (without the hockey pucks). And of course Naomi had saved her a table. But this time Doug ate with them. Well, not really with *them*, more like with Naomi.

It was cute to see the way they talked and giggled with each other, and it made TJ glad. Though she still could have done without Doug's

sniff-sniff-sniff-ing

and Naomi's continual

click-ing, *clack*-ing,

and

crunch-ing

Still, the two had proven themselves good friends. Not because they were anything great on the outside. But because they were something great inside.

click, *CLACK*,

crunch!

sniff-Sniff-sniff

Way inside.

Then there was Hesper Breakahart. The good news was the Acme Thought Broadcaster quit working. The bad news was everybody's memory didn't. Which explains why she now sat at a table all by herself.

"Doesn't anybody want to sit here?" she cried.

"I'm Hesper Breakahart, remember? The one you all love and adore. Hel-*lo*?!"

Everyone was doing their best to ignore her. Not an easy task, but somehow they managed.

"Okay, fine! You just wait till the reporters start coming back. And they will. You'll all come back! Just you wait!"

And finally there were Tuna and Herby. As usual, they were invisible to everybody but TJ. This time they floated above the table directly in front of her.

"Don't you guys have to get back and fix your time-travel thingy?" she whispered.

Tuna nodded. "That is correct. However, we wanted to make certain you were safe."

"And that you've, like, totally learned your lesson," Herby added.

"About not showing favoritism?" TJ whispered.

Herby nodded. "The best dudes and dudettes don't always come in the best packages."

"Like us," Tuna agreed.

Herby sucked in his stomach. "Speak for yourself."

TJ sighed. "Yeah, I get it. I really get it."

"Good." Tuna nodded. "Excellent. We shall then transport back to your home and resume working on our time-travel pod."

"Cool," Herby said as he pulled out his Swiss Army Knife.

TJ stiffened in fear, and Herby laughed. "Don't worry, Your Babe-ness. This is just our transporter. It never zworks on us." With that, he opened a blade and

chugga-**chugga**-chugga

BLING

Herby, Tuna, and TJ were transported to a busy

HONK-**HONK**

SQUEEEEEEEEAL!

freeway.

TJ spun around to see a giant semi racing at them. "Herby!"

"Sorry!" Herby shook the blade and

chugga-**chugga**-chugga

BLING

the three of them were in the middle of Antarctica, surrounded by a thousand penguins.

"Guys!"

chugga-*chugga*-chugga

BLING

And just like that, TJ was back in the cafeteria. Not only that, but Tuna and Herby had vanished. Now, at last, everything was completely normal . . . except for the baby penguin squirming inside her pocket.

"Guys!" she shouted. "GUYS!"

Everyone in the cafeteria turned to see who she was yelling at. But, of course, no one was there. Which meant that, once again, her face was turning beet red. And once again, she caught Chad looking at her from across the room.

She gave him a weak, pathetic smile.

He returned it, and for that she was glad. She would have been gladder if his eyes didn't say he still thought she had some major mental issues.

But that's how it was, and there was nothing she could do about it . . . at least for now.

Still, tomorrow would be a new day. A new day to start over with a fresh, clean slate. A new day where everything would be better. At least that's what she told herself. But she still had a few doubts.

Actually, with Tuna and Herby stuck in her life, she had some majorly major doubts.

Turn the page for a sneak peek at

AAAARGH!

the next wacky adventure in the TJ and
the Time Stumblers series by Bill Myers.

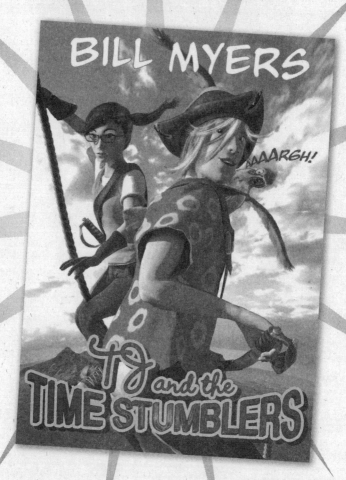

CHAPTER ONE

Beginnings . . .

TIME TRAVEL LOG:
Malibu, California, October 19

Begin Transmission:
Time-travel pod still zworked. Subject is growing
used to our presence. She barely groans when she
sees us. Big-time improvement. Currently assisting
her in studies, though she doesn't exactly appear
grateful.

End Transmission

"WHAT ARE YOU DOING?!" TJ Finkelstein yelled

as she dropped the book she was reading and jumped up from her desk. "HERBY!"

Now, TJ really wasn't a yeller. But when your room is suddenly filled with two dozen pirates from the 1700s (and none of them are as cute as Johnny Depp), well, that's enough to make anybody a little irritable.

Actually, it wasn't the pirates that bothered TJ as much as their

cling-clang

clunk!

sword fighting.

"TUNA!?" she shouted.

And even that wasn't as bad as their

cling-clang

jab!

cling-clang

jab!

"AIIuIIuuH!"

falling down all wounded on her floor.

"Great!" she cried. "How am I going to get those bloodstains out of my carpet? HERBY!"

There was still no answer, except for the

"Hardee-har-har . . ."

of another pirate as he swung toward her on a rope.

She screamed and dropped to the floor as he flew past, missing her by inches. Scrambling back to her feet, she searched the room—ducking this sword, dodging that saber as the pirates continued to

Cling-clang

clunk!

Once again she shouted, "TUNA! HERBY! WHERE ARE YOU?!"

Suddenly two frightened heads popped out from under her bed. The good news was the heads were still attached to their bodies. (With all the swinging

swords and sabers, that *was* good news.) The first
belonged to Herby. He had long blond bangs and
was not the brightest candle on the birthday cake.
(Sometimes he couldn't even find the party.) The
second belonged to Tuna, who had red hair and was
sort of chubby. They were both a couple years older
than TJ and perfectly normal . . . except for the part
about them coming from the 23rd century.

The 23rd century?!

That's right. And don't worry about the shouting—
that was TJ's first reaction too. It was also her second
reaction and her third . . . and her reaction every
time she woke up in the morning to see them standing in line to use her bathroom. (Apparently even
23rd-century time travelers need to use the facilities.)

It seems she was the subject of their history project back at their school. Someday she would grow
up to be a brilliant leader doing brilliant things (hard
to believe, since she was still having a hard time
opening her locker).

Anyway, the two boys had traveled back to her
time to observe her.

The only problem was they got stuck. Their time-
travel pod broke down and ran out of fuel. And
until they could fix it, TJ Finkelstein had become
their reluctant hostess. It wasn't bad enough that

she'd just moved to California from a small town in Missouri. Or that the kids at Malibu Junior High were the richest (and snobbiest) in the world. She also had to deal with all the catastrophes created by her brain-deprived friends from the 23rd century.

"What are you doing?" she demanded.

Tuna (aka Thomas Uriah Norman Alphonso the Third) cleared his throat. "You appeared to be having some difficulty with your *Treasure Island* book report."

"It's due tomorrow, and I haven't had a chance to—"

"Step lively, mateys! Comin' through!"

The boys ducked back under the bed and TJ jumped aside as two pirates rolled a heavy black cannon up to her window. She could only stare in disbelief.

Herby was the first to pop back out. Flipping his bangs to the side, he explained, "We figured the coolest way to read a book is to, like, live it."

TJ glanced around. "You mean to *watch* it, like a movie."

Suddenly a gnarled hand reached around and covered her mouth, while another shoved an old-fashioned pistol into her side. Her eyes widened in terror as she turned to see a pirate with a wooden leg and a parrot perched on his shoulder.

"Uh, no," Tuna corrected, "we mean to actually live it."

The pirate growled, "And who might ye be, missy? Someone out to steal me treasure?"

"Pieces of eight!" the parrot squawked. **"Pieces of eight!"**

Of course TJ screamed: "Mmumoumrrmform-mumrormf!" (Which might have sounded more like *"Excuse me, I'd appreciate not dying at this particular time in my life!"* if his hand weren't still over her mouth.)

"Are you saying you wish for us to stop?" Tuna asked.

TJ glared at him.

"I think we should take that as a yes," Herby said.

TJ gave a huge nod.

"Well, all right, if you're certain." Tuna pulled out a giant Swiss Army Knife (the type sold at time-travel stores everywhere). He opened the blade labeled Story Amplifier and

Zibwa-Zibwa-zibwa

absolutely nothing happened. (Well, except for the cool sound.)

"Try it again, dude!" Herby shouted.

Tuna shut the blade and reopened it. Again, nothing happened, except for the still very cool

Zibwa-zibwa-zibwa

Meanwhile, one of the pirates with the cannon at the window shouted, "Stand by!"

His partner produced a giant wooden match and yelled, "Standing by!"

Only then did TJ notice that the cannon wasn't just pointing out her window. It was pointing out her window directly at her neighbor Chad Steel's bedroom!

"Nuummmermumblemuffin!" she shouted. Only this time she made her point clearer by raising her foot high in the air and stomping hard onto the pirate's one good foot.

"ARGH!" he shouted, letting her go and jumping up and down on his other foot (which, unfortunately, was not there). So, having only a peg for a foot, he did a lot more

ker-plop-ing

onto the ground than jumping. And with all the
ker-plop-ing came a lot more *"ARGH!"*-ings followed
by a ton of *"Bleep-bleep-bleep, bleep-bleep-bleep"*-ings
(which is all pirates are allowed to scream in a
PG-rated book).

Meanwhile, the other two pirates were preparing
to fire the cannon.

"Ready!" the first pirate shouted.

TJ raced to the window. "Don't shoot! Don't
shoot!" She turned to the boys still under the bed.
"Tuna! Herby! Do something!"

"As you have no doubt observed," Tuna explained,
"our equipment is once again experiencing technical
difficulties."

"Ready!" the second pirate echoed his partner's
command as he struck the giant match. But before
he could light the cannon's fuse, TJ spun around and
blew it out.

He frowned. "What ye be doin' that for, missy?"

She twirled back to Tuna and Herby. "Hit it
on the ground again! Hit the knife thingy on the
ground!"

Once again the pirate lit a match and once again
she spun around and blew it out.

"ARGH," the pirate *argh*-ed. (He would have

thrown in a few *bleep*s of his own but figured his mother might be reading this book.)

Tuna called back to TJ, "I fail to see how hitting the knife upon the—"

"It's worked before!" Herby shouted at Tuna. "Give it a try."

The second pirate struck a third match, and this time blocking TJ from it, he managed to light the fuse. It started smoking and sputtering.

Tuna continued arguing with Herby. "I fail to see the logic in *thwack*-ing the Story Amplifier on the ground."

"Guys!" TJ shouted.

"That's how we fixed it before, dude."

"Guys!" TJ whirled back to the fuse, watching it burn toward the cannon.

"This is extremely expensive equipment," Tuna argued. "Such handling would be foolish and—"

"Aim!" the first pirate shouted.

"Aim!" the second pirate repeated as he adjusted the cannon so it would clearly destroy Chad's house.

"Fire!"

"Fire!"

Both men plugged their ears and closed their eyes . . . which gave TJ just enough time to throw herself at the cannon and *grrr, arrrr,* **ugghhh . . .**

move it 6¼ inches before it finally

k-blewie-ed

The good news was the cannonball missed Chad's house by mere inches. (Close, but when it comes to total demolition of a neighbor's house, every inch counts.)

The better news was Tuna finally agreed to

thwack, **thwack,** *thwack*

the knife on the floor until the Story Amplifier

Zibwa-Zibwa-zibwa

DING!

finally shut down.

Suddenly everything in the room was back to normal. No fighting pirates, no shooting cannons. Everything was gone . . . well, except for one or two parrot feathers floating to the ground and the gentle sound of

whhhhhuuuuuuUUUUU . . .

a light evening breeze blowing through the new hole in TJ's bedroom wall. The new hole that was roughly the size of a very large cannonball.

* * * * *

It had been a rough day for Hesper Breakahart, too. Besides the usual problems that came with being a super-rich, super-spoiled, and super-famous TV star on the Dizzy Channel, she had a terrible headache. There were three whiny reasons for her suffering:

WHINY REASON #1
The thirteen-year-old beauty queen had found a split end in her perfectly styled and perfectly blonde (because it was perfectly dyed) hair.

But that catastrophe was nothing compared to

WHINY REASON #2
Hesper had nearly broken a nail—which is a danger you risk when your PTB (Personal Tooth

Brusher) calls in sick and you have to brush your
teeth by yourself.

But even that was small potatoes (or in Hesper's
case, very small portions of caviar) when compared to

WHINY REASON #3

She was still having to talk to the common
people. (Insert gasp here.) That's right, the great
Hesper Breakahart, star of stage, screen, and her
own ego, actually had to pretend to like her fellow
students.

It had all started last week when the new girl
from Memphis—or Miami or whatever that Midwest
state that starts with an *M* is called—embarrassed
her in front of the entire school. For five terrifying
minutes, every student at Malibu Junior High had
heard Hesper's real thoughts broadcast through the
school's PA system. Now they *all* knew how much
she loathed them. (It's not that Hesper was a snob,
but when you're as big a winner as she is, it's hard to
ignore how big a loser everyone else is.)
So for the last week, she'd had to go around
school telling those awful, average people how much

she respected them (insert second gasp here). Talk
about embarrassing. Talk about humiliating. It was
almost as bad as when she had to share the cover of
Teen Idol with some stupid brother band that everyone was all gaga over.

But now it was

PAYBACK TIME

Hesper Breakahart was going to think up a plan
so nasty and so evil that TB—or BLT or whatever that
new girl's name was—would wish she'd never been
born.

"So what will it be?" Hesper's very best friend
since forever asked while sitting at Hesper's feet.
(All of Hesper's subjects—er, friends—sat at her feet.
Usually around the pool, working on their tans.)

"I don't know," Hesper said, drawing her perfectly
plucked eyebrows into a perfectly plucked frown.

"Make her drink regular tap water?" Hesper's
other very best friend since forever asked. (When
you're a TV star, you've got plenty of very best
friends.)

"Take away her credit cards?" another very best
friend asked.

"Make it so she can't get a pedicure for a whole month?"

All the girls shuddered.

"EEEEeeeeewWW . . ."

"Oh, I know; I know," the first very best friend said.

Hesper turned to her. "Yes, er, um . . ."

"Elizabeth."

Hesper flashed her recently whitened, glow-in-the-dark-teeth smile. "Yes, of course it is. What's on your mind, um, er . . ."

"Elizabeth."

"Right."

Elizabeth didn't need Hesper to know her name. Just letting her hang at the pool and breathe the same air was enough. "You know how weird stuff seems to be happening whenever the new kid is around?"

"Yes," another very best friend since forever said, "like the book that flew across Mr. Beaker's class when she came into the room?"

Another very best friend (I told you she had plenty) added, "Or that dodgeball that made a U-turn and hit you when she was in PE?"

"Or how 'bout when she—?"

"Please, please." Hesper held up her perfectly manicured hand. "Must we always be talking about her?"

Elizabeth frowned. "But I thought—"

"We were talking about what *I* was going to do to her."

"Oh, right." Elizabeth glanced down, embarrassed. If there was one thing you didn't talk about when you were around Hesper Breakahart, it was other people.

Hesper reached out an understanding hand and patted Elizabeth on the head. "That's okay, um, er, whoever you are."

Another very best friend since forever spoke up. "What if *you* hired a private detective?"

Hesper turned to her, waiting for more.

"*You* could have him find some dirt on her for *you,* and then *you* could tell everybody what *you* learned."

"*I* could?" Hesper asked. She was already liking the plan. (Well, not so much the plan as the *star* of the plan.) "But where would *I* find a detective to do that for *me*?"

Elizabeth's hand shot up in the air. "I could do it! I could do it!"

Hesper scowled.

Immediately, Elizabeth realized her error. "That is, for *you*. I could do it for *you* so *you* could tell everybody what *you* learned."

"Hmm . . ." A smile slowly crept around the corners of Hesper's all-too-perfect lips. "I like that . . . what's-your-name. Yes, I like that a lot."